Praise for *As Red As Blood* by Salla Simukka

"Limned in stark red, white, and black, this cold,
delicate snowflake of a tale sparkles with icy magic."
—*Kirkus Reviews* (Starred Review)

"Simukka creates a tough, self-sufficient heroine
in 17-year-old Lumikki Andersson in this first
book in the Snow White Trilogy . . . Fans of
Nesbø and Larsson won't be disappointed."
—*Publishers Weekly* (Starred Review)

"[A] YA novel in the tradition of Nordic noir—
edgy crime novels set in frigid lands."
—*Booklist* (Starred Review)

"A compelling start, a strong female character, the
rich background setting of Finland, and a hint of a
Snow White retelling are highlights of this work."
—*School Library Journal*

"The Arctic setting of this import is used to full
advantage, evoking a chilling mood and strewing
genuine frigid weather obstacles in Lumikki's
way . . . The first entry in Simukka's Snow White
trilogy will tempt mystery readers back for more."
—*The Bulletin of the Center for Children's Books*

AS
BLACK
AS
EBONY

ALSO BY SALLA SIMUKKA
As Red as Blood
As White as Snow

AS
BLACK
AS
EBONY

BOOK 3 IN THE SNOW WHITE TRILOGY

SALLA SIMUKKA

Translated from the Finnish
OWEN F. WITESMAN

SKYSCAPE

SKYSCAPE

Text copyright © 2014 Salla Simukka
Translation © 2015 Owen F. Witesman
Published by agreement with Tammi Publishers and
Elina Ahlbäck Literary Agency, Helsinki, Finland.

Published by Skyscape, New York

www.apub.com

Amazon, the Amazon logo, and Skyscape are trademarks of Amazon.com, Inc., or its affiliates.

ISBN-13: 9781477829950
ISBN-10: 1477829954

Cover design by Jennifer Wang
Book design by Susan Gerber

Printed in the United States of America

For everyone who loves. For everyone who is alone.

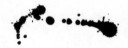

I've been watching you.

I've been watching you when you didn't know. I've been watching every move you make and every expression of your face. You thought you were invisible and unremarkable, but I have seen everything you do.

I know you better than anyone else. I know you better than yourself.

I know everything about you.

FRIDAY, DECEMBER 8

1

Lumikki awoke to a gaze.

A gaze aglow with warmth. It was hot, burning her skin and mind. The eyes were as familiar to Lumikki as her own. Light blue, the hue of ice and water and sky and light. Right now the eyes were smiling, although the gaze was steady and firm. A hand rose to stroke her hair and then continued in a light caress along the edge of her cheek to her neck. Lumikki felt a shudder of desire first in her belly and then below. Its grasp was so strong that she wasn't sure whether it felt dizzyingly good or agonizingly painful. She was ready in a heartbeat. Blaze could have done anything to her. She was open to everything, absolutely everything. She trusted Blaze and knew that whatever he did would bring pure pleasure. They made each other feel good because they only wanted the best for each other. Nothing less would do.

Blaze held his hand lightly on her neck and continued gazing. Lumikki could already feel herself throbbing and slick. Her breathing sped up. Her pulse pounded against Blaze's fingers. Leaning in, Blaze grazed her mouth with his, drawing his tongue teasingly along her lower lip, not kissing in earnest yet. Lumikki had to work to keep herself from grabbing Blaze with both hands and sucking his lips greedily. Finally, Blaze pressed his mouth gently against Lumikki's and began to kiss her just as irresistibly as he could. Lumikki would have groaned if she could make any sound. She closed her eyes and abandoned herself without reservation.

Suddenly, the kissing changed, becoming softer, tender, more tentative. It wasn't Blaze kissing her anymore. Lumikki opened her eyes, and the person kissing her drew away slightly. Lumikki looked him straight in the eyes.

Brown, friendly, happy eyes.

Sampsa's eyes.

"Good morning, Sleeping Beauty," Sampsa said and bent down to kiss Lumikki again.

"How old is that joke even?" Lumikki muttered as she stretched her arms, which felt numb.

"At least a hundred years."

Sampsa's laughter buzzed on Lumikki's neck. It tickled. It felt nice.

"Actually, it's much older than that. Perrault wrote down his version in the 1600s and the Grimms did theirs in the 1800s. But the story was being told a long time before then. Did you know that, in one of the older versions, the prince didn't wake Sleeping Beauty up with a gentle kiss at all? He raped her. And even that didn't wake her up until she gave birth to twins that . . ."

Sampsa had slipped his hand under the blanket and was caressing Lumikki's thighs, gradually moving toward her crotch. Lumikki was starting to have a hard time talking. The desire her dream had awoken was still pressing.

"Save the lectures for school," Sampsa whispered and then kissed her more insistently.

Lumikki stopped thinking about anything but Sampsa's lips and fingers. She didn't have a reason to think of anything else. Or anyone.

Sitting at the kitchen table, Lumikki looked at Sampsa's back as he brewed her espresso in a Moka Express and heated water for cocoa on another burner for himself. Sampsa had a nicely muscled, confident back. His plaid flannel pajama pants hung down just enough on his hips to show the two depressions between his buttocks and lower back. Lumikki restrained her desire to go rub her thumbs into them.

Sampsa's dark brown hair was mussed, and he was humming a folk song his group was practicing. They played modern folk music, and Sampsa was the group's violinist and lead singer. Lumikki had heard them play a couple of times at school assemblies. Not exactly her kind of music, but it was fast, happy, and energetic. For their genre, they were obviously quite good.

Early December sleet splashed against the kitchen windowpanes. Lumikki pulled her feet up onto her chair, wrapping her arms around them and resting her chin on her knees. At what point had it become perfectly normal to have a sweet, half-naked boy bustling about in the kitchen of her pathetic little studio apartment every morning?

It had all started at the beginning of the fall term, in mid-August. Maybe not right at the beginning, since for the first few days everyone in the school had wanted to talk to Lumikki and hear about the fire in Prague and how she saved the cult members who set it from committing suicide. How did it feel to be a hero? How did it feel to be famous? How did it feel to see her picture in all the magazines? Of course, the media in Finland had covered the story, and practically every newspaper wanted to interview Lumikki after she got home. But she had declined. And she'd handled her inquisitive schoolmates' questions by responding so briefly they grew bored with how little they were getting out of her.

Then Sampsa came. He had been in the same high school as Lumikki all along. Walked the same halls, sat in the same classrooms. Lumikki had known his name, but Sampsa had never been anything more than another face in the crowd.

One day, Sampsa sat down next to Lumikki in the cafeteria. He sought her out to chat before class and then walked her home as far as the square downtown. And he did it all as if it were the most natural thing in the world. Sampsa didn't pressure her or force himself into Lumikki's life. When a casual conversation reached a natural conclusion, he didn't try to drag it out. He never took offense at Lumikki's occasional, rather unfriendly rebuffs. Sampsa simply talked to her, looking at her with that friendly, open gaze of his, being present but knowing when to leave before the mood turned awkward.

Sampsa's every action said: "I don't expect anything from you. I don't hope for anything from you. I don't demand anything from you. You can be just how you are. I just think it's nice to spend time with you. My self-respect doesn't depend on you smiling at me, but I sure wouldn't mind if you did."

Gradually, Lumikki found herself looking forward to seeing Sampsa. She felt warm when he sat next to her and looked her straight in the eyes, sincerely and happily. Tiny butterflies began flitting around Lumikki's stomach when Sampsa's hand grazed hers.

They started getting together outside of school. To go on long walks, to drink coffee, to go to concerts. Lumikki felt like a feather carried by a gentle breeze into moments and situations that felt utterly natural and right. Hand in hand with Sampsa. The slightly fumbling yet warm first kiss one dark November evening. The hand that stroked her hair and back the first time he slept at her place. Sampsa was patient. He didn't try to lead Lumikki into doing anything she wasn't ready for.

Then, one night, Lumikki was ready. And she wasn't the slightest bit surprised that physical intimacy with Sampsa was just as good and safe and right as everything else with him.

By December, they were an official couple. Lumikki felt like things were the way they were supposed to be. She had finally fallen in love with someone new. She had gotten over Blaze and their breakup, even though it had taken a long time—more than a year. Blaze had disappeared completely from Lumikki's life when his gender reassignment process from physical girl to physical boy was at its most difficult. Blaze thought he couldn't be with anyone then, not even his beloved Lumikki, and he hadn't given her any option other than to accept that decision, even though she could never completely understand it.

But now, Sampsa was in her kitchen, brewing coffee and humming and generally making Lumikki want to kiss every vertebra in his spine.

This was life. Life was good.

It didn't even matter that sleet was buffeting the window so hard now that it almost sounded like someone was clawing the glass trying to get in.

2

Once upon a time, there was a key.

The key was metal, perfectly palm sized. On its head was a skillfully cast image of a heart. The key was forged in 1898. The same year a small chest was made, with a lock that fit the key. Over the decades, the surface of the key was burnished by the touch of human hands. The first person who held it was the metal smith who forged it. Then it made its way to the hands of the chest's first owner. He had seven children, all of whom held the key in turn. At that point, the key had been touched so many times already that identifying individual fingerprints was impossible.

The last time the key had been touched was more than fifteen years ago. Then, two people had held it, several times in turn. In their hands, the key had felt much heavier than it really was. And when they turned the key in the lock of the chest, they felt as if someone had twisted a sharp, serrated knife in their hearts. The last time the key had been touched, salty droplets fell on it.

Then the key was hidden. And it lay hidden, alone, abandoned year after year.

But not forgotten. There were two people in the world who thought of the key every day. It was forged into their minds and still burned like glowing iron. If their thoughts could have made the key shine, its scintillating light would have revealed its hiding place from miles away.

Once upon a time, there was a key that was hidden.

In stories, like in real life, everything hidden wants eventually to be found.

The key waited to be touched again and to open the chest. The key waited patiently, immobile and mute.

Its time would soon come.

3

This was Lumikki's forest. The branches were black shadows; the black shadows were branches. Tree roots coiled along the ground like snakes before diving underground to form a wide, thick network curling around each other, the veins of different trees uniting beneath the soil, drinking from the same life force. The branches up above traced their own map between the trees and toward the sky with so many lines that light struggled to find a route through. The branches were arms, brush strokes, and hair. Some thin, some delicate. Some thick, some strong. All beautiful.

The forest was a game of shadows, a dance of dim light and mist, hushed whispers and sighs, passing currents of air that gave her goose bumps. All of the shadow creatures, dream animals, sneaking beasts, and darkness dwellers bade Lumikki welcome. She was with her kind again.

The blackness settled around and inside Lumikki, at once familiar and foreign. She ran more freely in the forest. She breathed deeper. The ribbons holding her hair came undone and her braids fell out with the sylvan wind seizing her hair and doing with it what it would. Twigs and leaves clung to her locks. The fabric of Lumikki's silk dress ripped. Branches scratched her arms. She smelled the soil and decomposing leaves. Lumikki's eyes focused, and she saw the smallest movements of the shadows. There was blood on her hands, drying quickly and turning black like the soil. Trying to wash it away would be futile. It would stay on her hands always, because Lumikki was a killer, a predator.

This was Lumikki's forest. In its darkness was room for passion and fear, despair and joy. The air that filled her lungs was heady. In the embrace of the forest, she grew into something whole. She became more than herself, more free. Lumikki settled down to lie on the roots, pressing her palm against the damp earth and wishing that she could become part of the roots, merging with them and penetrating the earth to find the heart spring.

The forest sighed and throbbed around Lumikki as if it had one single pulse. Her pulse.

———————

"Okay, good! That bit about the heart is a perfect way to end the scene."

Tinka's voice snapped Lumikki out of whatever state she had been in and she sat up on the stage. She felt like she had just woken up from a deep sleep. This scene in the play always affected her that way. She got so into it that, for a moment, she forgot that she was in the high school's small auditorium rehearsing a play. They were calling it *The Black Apple.*

Lumikki still wasn't sure whether agreeing to act in the play had been a good idea. Sampsa was the one who talked her into it.

"Hey, it's a new take on 'Snow White.' With a name like yours, how could you pass that up? The Snow White role was practically written for you," Sampsa had said, smiling that happy, encouraging smile that Lumikki'd do just about anything to see.

She had been ready to take part in a play, although the thought of playing her kinda-sorta namesake felt a bit self-aggrandizing. It was bad enough that half the people she met felt compelled to make dumb jokes about her fairy-tale first name. Tinka, who had written the play and was also directing it, only needed a couple of rehearsals to convince Lumikki that the script was actually pretty great and the production was going to be fantastic. Tinka had just started at the arts high school that fall, but she had enough chutzpah to direct students two years older than her.

On the outside, Tinka was a stereotypical artsy student with her eclectic, constantly changing clothing and hairstyles. One day she might come to school in a tutu with her red hair braided in a bun; the next day in boots, ripped jeans, and an oversized hoodie with her hair in a rat's nest; then a third day in a three-piece suit and a bowler hat. Variety and fickleness weren't an attempt to get attention for Tinka, though, and she wasn't putting on an act. She was direct, down-to-earth, and determined in a way that Lumikki admired.

The Black Apple opened with the prince gazing at Snow White lying in her glass casket, burning with love for the beautiful, motionless maid. Then they began transporting the casket to the prince's castle and, on the way, one of the bearers tripped, jostling the casket, which made the piece of poisoned apple dislodge from Snow White's throat, allowing her to wake up. So, up to this point, the plot followed the classic fairy tale. However, in Tinka's play, when Snow White awoke from her poison coma, she wasn't thrilled about her role as the prince's bride-to-be. She was used to the forest, to its shadows and beasts. She didn't want to move to a golden castle to have servants wait on her hand and foot. A queen had too little freedom to do as she pleased. Besides, the prince only worshiped Snow White's beauty and wasn't interested in her mind.

Tinka's play had strong feminist overtones, but it wasn't preachy or didactic. It was just intense and disturbing. None of the characters in *The Black Apple* was purely virtuous. Not even the Huntsman, who did try to save Snow White, but was motivated by his own desires and aspirations too.

Sense by sense, Lumikki returned to the ordinary, real world surrounding her. Recovering from the last act always took some time. It was a powerful, hypnotic scene: Lumikki lay on the ground. The lights went dark. For a moment, the stage and house were in perfect blackness with the sound a heartbeat echoing louder and louder. Just before this, Lumikki had learned of the Huntsman's death and killed the prince with a sharp silver hair comb. Then she fled the castle back to her beloved forest, to the company of the darkness and shadows and beasts.

When they'd rehearsed the scene for the first time with all of the props, sound effects, and lighting, no one had been able to say a word for a long time afterward. They just glanced at each other as if asking, "Did you feel that too? Were we just somewhere else?"

"Next run-through on Monday night. Same time, same place!" Tinka reminded them.

"Aren't we about ready now? How about we take a night off?" suggested Aleksi, who was playing the prince.

Tinka cast him a scornful glance.

"We have two weeks until opening night and a ton of work left to do. And some people still need to learn their lines all the way through."

Aleksi shrugged and started trudging out of the auditorium.

Sampsa came over to Lumikki and stroked her back.

"You were really good. Again."

"Thanks," Lumikki replied as she tied the laces of her combat boots.

Her hands were still trembling slightly from the intensity of the scene.

"See you tomorrow. I gotta run. I'm already late and my mom's gonna kill me."

Sampsa kissed Lumikki's forehead, threw his backpack over his shoulder, and left. The last couple of scenes had given him time to change out of his huntsman costume already. Every Friday night, his whole family got together for dinner, including Sampsa's grandparents and an aunt who lived in Tampere. They had been doing it for years, so Sampsa didn't feel like he could skip out. He'd invited Lumikki a couple of times, but so far she had declined. The thought of the way everyone would stare as they sized her up was unpleasant. Lumikki had promised to come for coffee on Sunday though, when only Sampsa's parents and little sister would be home. That sounded like more than enough for her.

The dark, deserted school lay in a drowsy silence as Lumikki and Tinka walked down the stairs to the mirrored front lobby. The halls looked strange empty, and their steps echoed. During the day, they were crammed with students and the decibel level exceeded industrial safety limits.

Tinka was analyzing the problems with each scene of the play, but Lumikki couldn't concentrate on what she was saying. Had agreeing to act in the play been a mistake? She didn't like how much she lost herself in her role and how the real world disappeared around her. She wasn't pretending to be Snow White running through the forest. She was Snow White running through the forest, feeling and smelling blood on her hands. Snow White's pulse was Lumikki's pulse. Lumikki wasn't used to that kind of loss of self-control, and it frightened her.

Eventually, Tinka noticed Lumikki's distance, and they donned their coats in silence. Around her neck, Lumikki wrapped the heavy, red wool scarf her former classmate Elisa had made for her and sent in the mail. They still kept in touch. Last winter, Lumikki never could have guessed Elisa would become a true friend.

Outside, it was snowing large, fluffy flakes that melted the instant they touched the black ground. No hope yet that December would turn out white.

"Some of the cast might be a little checked out still, but at least you aren't. You're killing it," Tinka said as they walked through the schoolyard gates.

Then she waved and headed in the opposite direction from Lumikki, who didn't manage to get out anything sensible in reply. Mud squelched under Lumikki's boots as she turned toward downtown. Farther along the path, she saw the school psychology teacher and one of the math teachers, who had apparently been working late too. This time of year, the teachers tended to work long hours grading tests and essays. Some of them preferred not to take their work home, staying at school late into the evening instead. In a way, it was nice seeing them outside of school, chatting and laughing together. Even so, Lumikki was happy to be far enough behind them not to be able to make out any of their words. She thought it was best to know as little as possible about her teachers' private lives.

The illuminated red brick tower of the Alexander Church rose into the sky, stately and familiar. It was so dark that the few old gravestones in the churchyard were invisible from the path. The large snowflakes looked like feathers against the black branches of the trees. Fallen from the wings of angels. Lumikki pushed her hands deeper into her coat pockets and walked faster.

In her left pocket, she felt the rustle of something strange, something that didn't belong there. Lumikki pulled it out. It was a white sheet of paper, folded four times. Lumikki opened it fold by fold to find a short letter typed on a computer. She stopped under a street lamp to read it.

My Lumikki,

Your prince doesn't know you. Not in the play and not in real life. He only sees your outer shell. He only sees a part of you. I see deeper, into your soul.

You have blood on your hands, Lumikki. You know it. I know it.

I see every move you make.

You will hear from me again soon. But know this: If you tell anyone about my messages, one single person, there will soon be much more blood. Then no one will survive the opening night of your play.

With love,

Your admirer, your Shadow

Lumikki gasped and she looked up from the letter. Something flickered at the edge of her field of vision. Something black.

But when she looked toward it, she saw nothing but the long, dreary shadows of the trees.

4

Alla kvällar lät prinsessan smeka sig.
Men den som smeker stillar blott sin egen hunger
och hennes längtan var en skygg mimosa,
en storögd saga inför verkligheten.
Nya smekningar fyllde hennes hjärta med bitter sötma
och hennes kropp med is, men hennes hjärta ville ännu
    mer.
Prinsessan kände kroppar, men hon sökte hjärtan;
hon hade aldrig sett ett annat hjärta än sitt eget.

(Every evening, the princess allowed herself to be caressed.
But the caresser only satisfied his own hunger,
while her desire was a shy mimosa,

a wide-eyed fairy tale in the face of reality.
New caresses filled her heart with a bitter flush
and her body with ice, but her heart wanted more.
The princess knew bodies, but she sought hearts;
she had never seen any heart but her own.)

Lumikki read "The Princess" quietly to herself. The words calmed her. She had read her copy of Edith Södergran's posthumously released collection *The Land Which Is Not* so many times she knew every poem practically by heart. The first words always brought back the rest of the lines. Familiar poems were like mantras. Their calming effect rested on the way the words flowed one after another in just the right order, without any surprises.

Lumikki couldn't go straight home after reading the letter. Was someone really following her every step? She'd tried to rationalize away the fear. In all likelihood, the letter was just a bad joke. Black humor. A cruel game. Someone somewhere was laughing right now thinking about how frightened she would be, but soon they'd jump out and reveal the truth. Gotcha!

But what if the letter was real? What if she really did have a crazy stalker who was prepared to kill people? Lumikki couldn't risk treating the letter too cavalierly. Her life experience had left her little doubt that people were capable of evil deeds. She'd endured years of brutal school bullying and then seen up close the ruthlessness of the international drug trade. Just that past summer in Prague, she had seen a charismatic leader use fear to manipulate his religious cult into attempting mass suicide.

All her life was missing was a deranged stalker, Lumikki thought with a bitter snort.

The sounds around her were pleasantly muffled. Calm footsteps, the rustling of pages, hushed conversations. Lumikki knew that if she went and sat by the base of one of the arches that made up the roof, she'd be able to make out every word being said at the base of the other side of the arch. Reima and Raila Pietilä had designed the Tampere City Library that way. However, Lumikki didn't want to hear anyone else's private conversations right now. She wanted to be wrapped in the protective familiarity of the library's indistinct murmurs, surrounded by people but still alone so she could calm down and build up the courage to go home. The library was only a two-minute walk from the Alexander Church.

Lumikki had always found the building's undulating dome and avian plume of arches soothing inside and out. There was just enough walking space between the shelves, but if you wanted, you could hide in them. The library was full of round reading tables and secret nooks where no one ever bothered you.

Lumikki wanted to text Sampsa and ask him to come over for the night after his family dinner. No matter how late that would be. But she had never done something like that before, so Sampsa might wonder. And then Lumikki would have to lie, and she didn't want to lie to Sampsa.

No, she would have to make it through the night alone. Then she would have to find out as soon as possible who put the letter in her pocket. She'd have to do that alone too.

Lumikki had thought she wasn't going to be so alone anymore. She had thought wrong. Suddenly, she felt that familiar emptiness and desolation filling her inside. She was always alone, in the end. Lumikki stared at the stanzas of the poem, unable to read any more.

Just then a deep, crisp scent of pine forest surrounded her and a warm hand gently brushed her neck.

"Edith Södergran. Are you reading our poems without me?"

Lumikki knew before she turned to look over her shoulder. She knew before the voice and the words. She knew from the smell and the touch.

Blaze.

He stood sideways behind Lumikki. Smiling. Real. He looked maybe a little more like a boy than he had eighteen months earlier. His hair was shorter and lighter, and there was a new calm and self-assurance in his posture, but otherwise he was exactly the same. Those ice-blue eyes were the same, and Lumikki sank into them instantly like breaking through a frozen crust as thin as thought and plunging into the black lake beneath.

A storm of emotions washed over Lumikki. She wanted to curl up in Blaze's arms as close as she could and tell him everything about the letter and how afraid she was and what had happened in the past year and all the longing and loneliness and dreams and black thoughts and ask him to protect her and save her from solitude and evil and take him home and tear off all his clothes and her own and get tangled up with him on the floor and kiss and kiss and kiss and press every hungry inch of her skin against him and burst into flames and forget herself and the world and that they were two different beings because front to front they were one, as seamless as could be with no boundaries, and Lumikki wanted to burn and burn and burn without fearing the fire for once.

Lumikki swallowed. A tremor ran through her. She couldn't speak.

"It's nice to see you. Wanna go get coffee? Or are you busy?" Blaze asked as if it were perfectly natural to chat like normal people.

"No," Lumikki managed to say.

"Good. Should we go upstairs to the cafe?"

"No. I mean we can't go get coffee." Blaze stared at Lumikki, a little confused, but then he smiled mischievously.

"We can do something else if you want to."

With trembling hands, Lumikki put her book back on the shelf and pulled her knitted cap down over her ears.

"No, we can't. I'm busy. I can't see you. Now." Lumikki heard the words coming out of her mouth, haltingly, breathlessly.

"Okay. Well, some other time then. Is your phone number the same? I'll call or text you."

Blaze's voice was warm and composed. Don't, Lumikki should have said. That was what she wanted to say. But she also didn't.

"I have to go. Bye."

Lumikki's legs wanted to run out of the library, as fast and as far as possible away from Blaze. But she forced herself to walk. Briskly and purposefully. Without looking back.

Not until she was outside in the fresh air did Lumikki realize she should have said she was dating someone.

She hadn't said it though, because after diving into the burning ice water of Blaze's eyes, she had forgotten that fact completely.

I love you.

    Three words that are so easy to say but so hard to mean. I mean them. I breathe each word and they become a part of me. I say them to you and they become a part of you. My love moves into you. It makes you burn even more beautiful, strong, and radiant.

    I make you brighter than the brightest star of the night-time sky.

    You become mine, completely. As was always meant to be. Because it is your fate. And mine.

SATURDAY, DECEMBER 9

5

Sister, sister, sister, sister.

The word pounded in Lumikki's head, as it always did now when she was visiting her parents in Riihimäki. It would just never come out of her mouth. Her mom had made goat cheese lasagna for lunch, which was one of Lumikki's favorites, but today she could barely taste it. Lumikki felt as if all of her pleasure centers had been numbed. Food was just necessary fuel. Even coffee didn't taste good.

Lumikki figured it was because of the letter. She was still convinced that it was just a nasty prank, but the message bothered her anyway, lurking somewhere behind her thoughts. It made colors grayer and covered the world in a thin haze. Tastes disappeared. If Lumikki could just figure out who the letter was from, she would get her revenge, which would be civilized but definitely served cold.

But at her parents' house, the only thing Lumikki could think about was that she still hadn't found out whether she really used to have a sister. The memories awakened in Prague by Lenka's lie had felt so real. She had been sure that she had once had a sister. Since returning to Finland, she wasn't as confident, though. She'd thought she would just slap the question down on the table as soon as she got home, but that hadn't happened.

When Lumikki had told her mom and dad about Lenka, she left out the part about Lenka claiming she was Lumikki's sister. Over the fall, Lumikki had exchanged a few e-mails with Lenka, who had started studying math, chemistry, and biology on her own, hoping eventually to get into medical school. Lenka had also subtly let Lumikki understand that she had never moved out of Jiři's apartment. Jiři had found a new job at a local paper. Lumikki had read between the lines that, after saving Lenka from the burning house with Lumikki, Jiři had found he liked taking care of Lenka. Lumikki was happy for them.

Sometimes, Lenka signed her e-mails "your sister in spirit." The word filled Lumikki's thoughts. But she avoided saying it out loud.

Why? Wouldn't it have been easiest just to talk about it? Lumikki didn't know what was holding her back.

Maybe it was something in her mom and dad's concern and earnestness, all the warmth and love they had shown since she returned from Prague. The uncharacteristic intimacy. The idea of interrogating them just felt wrong. Her dad's trip to Prague years ago had turned out to be just a coincidence without any connection to the sister issue at all, so Lumikki hadn't grilled them about that either.

To tell the truth, she had enjoyed all the warmth. She hadn't wanted to jeopardize it by talking about something that might have been only her imagination anyway. People could invent memories if they really wanted or if they thought that something had happened in the past.

Days without bringing it up had turned into weeks, and weeks had turned into months. Eventually, Lumikki realized that there wasn't any natural way to bring up the topic anymore. Her parents' burst of tenderness had subsided, and all three of them had returned to their old, familiar roles where they talked about general things, kept in touch just as much as necessary for it to seem normal, and tried to avoid too many awkward lulls in conversation during a Saturday lunch like this.

"Would you like some more?" her mother asked to fill one such silent pause.

"No, thank you," Lumikki replied. "Could I look at some of those old pictures though?"

"Again?" her dad asked. "You've already seen all of them."

"Yeah, but I've been thinking that I might be able to use them for a project at school," Lumikki explained.

"I'm going to make coffee," her mother said, clearing the plates just a little too hastily.

Lumikki sat on the living room sofa with the photo album, slowly turning pages. She knew every picture by heart. She had looked at them so many times, this fall especially. She had tried to find some solution in them, some key.

There was her mom and dad's wedding picture. Some pictures from a cottage in Åland. A couple of fuzzy shots of their home in Turku, where they lived until Lumikki was four. She only had dim memories of it. It was an idyllic, two-story wooden house in the Port Arthur area. Nothing like this stubby row house in Riihimäki. It seemed strange that they would have moved into a much less expensive house. For the price of their place in Turku, they should have been able to buy a big one here. Apparently, there were money problems no one had ever told Lumikki about.

"Why did we move from Turku?" Lumikki asked. Looking up from his newspaper, her father furrowed his brow.

"For work."

That explanation didn't make a lot of sense. Her father had always traveled for work, and most of his trips took him to Helsinki. And you would have thought library jobs for her mother would have been easier to find in a big city like Turku than a tiny town like Riihimäki. Lumikki didn't press the matter.

She wondered yet again why there were so few pictures. There were just a couple from each year of her life and most of them weren't very good. Not that Lumikki needed hundreds of baby pictures like people took nowadays, starting at the actual birth, but it was still strange for there to be this few. Lumikki had seen childhood photo albums at other people's houses, and they were always much thicker and there were usually more than one. Maybe her mom and dad had just never been interested in photography. Or maybe they hadn't been interested in taking pictures of Lumikki.

Lumikki paused longer on one picture than the others. In it, she was seven years old. She stood in the middle of a schoolyard. It was winter. She remembered Mom suddenly wanting to take a picture after dropping her off at school.

"Come on, smile!" her mom had said.

In the picture, Lumikki stared straight at the camera seriously, without the slightest hint of a smile. She simply didn't have any reason to grin in that place. The bullying had started that winter, and Lumikki had hated every day she had to go to school. Now she looked at the picture and saw the chilling fear behind her defiant gaze.

Lumikki never wanted her eyes to look that way again. But she recognized it all too often in the mirror even now.

Lumikki closed the album. It wasn't going to tell her anything new today. It wasn't going to reveal the secrets hidden in the past.

After coffee, her mother asked Lumikki, "Are you going to stay for a sauna tonight?"

The question was more rhetorical than a real invitation. It was the question you were supposed to ask.

"No. Schoolwork," Lumikki replied.

Just as she was expected to reply.

Walking to the railway station, Lumikki passed her old middle school. Seeing the building and the yard always brought the taste of iron to her mouth. Those had been the worst years of the violence and humiliation. The hitting and shouting. The isolation. All the lies to get Lumikki to come to school at the wrong time, to bring the wrong PE clothes, to do the wrong homework. She had tried to be careful and only believe what she had heard with her own ears from the teachers, but she had still been tricked time and time again. It was easy for the bullies to forge messages and get other kids to play along.

Just as nauseating was the memory of how she had finally risen up against her bullies, Anna-Sofia and Vanessa, brutally attacking them.

The rage. The loss of control. The hunger to kill.

Afterward, Lumikki didn't know whether she was more afraid of the bullies or herself. Everything she knew she was capable of and how it felt to want to take another person's life just to put an end to her personal hell. Lumikki wasn't proud of her feelings, but she also didn't try to deny them. That was why she had tried so hard to teach herself composure and self-control. She didn't intend to give other people the upper hand, but she also didn't want to act in anger.

At least Lumikki tried to make that her guiding rule. Following it wasn't always so easy.

Sunny memories of Riihimäki were few and far between for Lumikki. One of them was of the Riihimäki Theater where Lumikki had seen a play when she was nine. She couldn't remember what the play was anymore, but that didn't matter. Lumikki had loved the smell of the auditorium, the hush that replaced the hum of conversation in the audience, and the moment when the lights had dimmed but the performance had not yet begun. The sense of tension and expectation when everything was still possible.

Lumikki had sat right in the front row, obliging her to tilt back her head to see properly. The actors had been almost close enough to touch. Lumikki had been able to see even their slightest expressions.

Lumikki remembered one dark-haired actor dancing, jumping, and running especially lightly and effortlessly. The hem of her aquamarine skirt undulated like rolling seawater. When the actor jumped right to the edge of the stage though, Lumikki caught a glimpse of a knee brace under her skirt. After that, Lumikki started watching the actor's expressions more carefully, noticing under the winning smile and bubbly laughter and flowing words a hint of pain. With every jump and step of the dance, a shadow passed over the actor's face so subtly it probably didn't register for anyone else. It was like a fog fell over her eyes for a split second.

Lumikki watched the actor, spellbound. She forgot to watch the rest of the play. The plot wasn't interesting anymore. Lumikki stared at the changing shades of the actor's gray eyes, thinking. It was possible to take on a role no one else could see through. You could hide pain.

That carefree dancing and the laughter that filled the stage like apple blossoms had become a symbol of hidden strength and power for Lumikki. She thought that she could be like this actor someday too. She could choose her role and step onto the stage or sit in the audience. Lumikki could be anyone.

Seen from the window of her train home to Tampere, the December afternoon seemed to darken even more quickly than normal. It was gray. Just as gray as it had been for all of October, November, and the beginning of December. Today it wasn't sleeting, it was drizzling. The ground was black. The bare branches of the trees were black. Lumikki saw her reflection in the window. Her eyes looked black.

Fifteen minutes outside of Tampere, Lumikki had to go to the bathroom so badly that she decided to use the restroom in the train instead of waiting until getting home. When she returned to her place, a folded sheet of paper lay on her seat. Lumikki glanced around. No one else was in the car. Just then, the train pulled up to one of the Tampere suburb stations.

Lumikki unfolded the paper with trembling hands.

My Lumikki,

I know how bad it is for you walking past that building. I know what you went through there. And it makes me feel so furious on your behalf. If you wanted, I could make them suffer. If you wanted, I could paint the walls with their blood. I could finish what you started, your just revenge. One word from you and I would do it.

I know their names. Anna-Sofia and Vanessa. Don't think I'm not serious.

And since we're talking about names, I know other names too. You are Lumikki, Snow White, but

*do you remember that there was once someone almost
like Briar Rose?*

*Remember. You'll find her name. You haven't
forgotten it even if you might have forgotten
everything else.*

I'm always following you.

Your Shadow

Bile rose in Lumikki's throat. Whoever had left the note, there was no way he was on the train anymore. He would have gotten off at that stop. The stalker's timing had been perfect.

The thought that whoever wrote this had followed her to Riihimäki, kept watch to know when she was coming back, and waited to see whether she would go to the bathroom nauseated Lumikki. All just to be able to leave her this anonymous message.

This wasn't a practical joke.

And no one could know the things this note said. There were things Lumikki had never told anyone. Things like the names of her tormentors.

Lumikki could barely dial her phone, her hands were shaking so much.

Thankfully, Sampsa answered immediately.

"Can I see you today?" Lumikki asked, trying to sound nonchalant.

"No."

Lumikki swallowed.

"Why not?"

"I have band practice tonight and I've got an important project to finish, namely buying you a Christmas present," Sampsa said with a laugh. "So you'll have to wait until tomorrow, beautiful."

"Okay."

Lumikki would have liked to draw out the conversation and hold on to the safe warmth of Sampsa's voice, but she didn't dare say anything that might reveal everything wasn't alright. So she made small talk, telling him about her parents' vacation plans and remodeling plan. The sort of chitchat Lumikki never indulged. But Sampsa was in a hurry, so soon Lumikki was sitting with a mute phone in her hand, staring at her reflection in the window.

In her eyes was the same defiant fear as when she was seven years old.

6

Every hit and every kick had to strike the opponent in a way that significantly reduced his fighting effectiveness. Halfhearted attacks were pointless. They just consumed energy without helping to vanquish your enemy.

Lumikki squeezed her fingers into a fist. Left, left, right. Left, left, right. And remember to block. Keep moving.

How blood starts flowing from a nose when it comes into contact with a fist. How a cheekbone breaks when a sharp kick hits it. The opponent's legs give way. He falls. He is at your mercy.

Suddenly, Lumikki couldn't go on. Her feet wouldn't budge. The others continued moving to the thumping music of the Combat session, following the trainer's shouted commands, but Lumikki couldn't aim another single strike at her imaginary foe. Of course, this was just aerobics, a group exercise class spiced up with a little faux martial arts, but right now the mental images were too much.

Before her eyes, Lumikki saw Anna-Sofia and Vanessa lying in the snow, beaten to within an inch of their lives. No, that hadn't really happened, but she still imagined it that way. Was "Shadow" right? Did she still want revenge on those girls?

Lumikki had thought that coming to Combat would take her mind off the notes, but that hadn't happened. The music thundered in the gym. The air stank of sweat. A few others started casting irritated glances at Lumikki because she was just standing in the middle of the room, resting her arms on her knees. *Get out of the way*, their eyes said.

As soon as her legs felt like they would carry her, Lumikki started weaving her way through the crowd. She didn't even bother saying sorry when she bumped into a few of the other girls enthusiastically hitting and kicking at the air. After making it to the locker room, Lumikki headed straight for the toilet. She barely got the door latched and the lid up before the vomit gushed out of her mouth. Lumikki held the sides of the bowl, retching pieces of goat cheese lasagna. Her whole body shook.

Lumikki didn't remember when she had last thrown up. It felt just as horrible as ever.

In the shower, Lumikki was alone. She could still hear the Combat class outside. Coming here had been a bad idea. She would have to find some other way to clear her mind. Lumikki stood under the warm water long after all of the shampoo and soap was rinsed from her hair and skin. The wetness of the water was a caress. It was an embrace she could take momentary refuge in.

Lumikki tried to pinpoint the department store speakers playing the saccharine song. She hoped that if she could cast them a sufficiently searing glance, the worst Christmas ditty in the history of kitsch would end as the speakers burst into flames. Wham! released "Last Christmas" in 1984. Wasn't it about time for it to crawl off to the pop song graveyard and die?

Apparently, department stores thought differently. Maybe somewhere someone had done a study and found that of all the horrible Christmas songs ever written, this was the one that made people spend the most. The bitterness and pain of a broken heart, the desire for revenge, and the thought that, this Christmas, I'll give my gifts to someone special who knows how to value them. I'll buy the most beautiful ones. I'll buy the most expensive ones. I'll prove my love with such a big pile of cash that no one will be able to doubt the sincerity of my feelings. But at the same time, those shoppers relishing the singer's bittersweet wistfulness, knowing his broken heart still beats for the one who shattered it.

Lumikki hated this song. She hated the pre-Christmas rush. The real and imagined glitter that rested on everything was meant to mimic snow, but really looked more like sugar frosting. The Christmas of department stores was the one you saw in American romantic comedies where they condensed a lifetime of sappy love and togetherness into a few winter days when everything was perfect just so long as the sets and props were just so. There was a fire in the hearth and mistletoe and glittering gold and fake snow and an enormous mountain of perfectly chosen presents piled and a full Christmas dinner and fuzzy socks and handmade chocolates and Christmas carols and the scent of cinnamon and ginger and everything so perfect you could almost gag.

That was the Christmas dream the department stores sold, and the Tampere Stockmann was no exception.

Lumikki also hated buying Christmas presents because it felt so fake. She would prefer to give gifts when she felt like it, no matter what the date was. Buying Christmas presents was a ritual you had to perform because it was expected. Lumikki knew she couldn't not buy Sampsa a present. But she also knew the distress she would feel the moment she received some beautiful, carefully chosen, thoughtful gift and all she had for him was something pointless and impersonal she had bought in a panic. Because Lumikki had already noticed Sampsa was a gift giver. By some incredible instinct, the boy had already managed to give her the perfect necklace, a simple silver chain with a small black stone pendant; the world's best notebook; and a pair of half-finger gloves Lumikki always wore at home when a cold gale was blowing through the chinks in the window.

Sampsa gave his gifts lightly, without making a big deal about it. He gave gifts the way the best gifts were given, without the slightest expectation of receiving anything in return. He knew how to do it in a way that the other person never felt indebted or guilty. Lumikki respected that so much, but she knew she couldn't skip Christmas.

Right now, it also felt necessary to be surrounded by all these painfully bright lights and exhaustingly cheery songs. To shut the stalker's letters out of her mind. Lumikki didn't know what she should do about them, and because she couldn't stand uncertainty, she tried to forget about it. At least for a while. Maybe her subconscious was working on a solution.

"What is up with all this chintzy crap?" a voice asked behind Lumikki.

Turning, Lumikki saw Tinka and Aleksi. It was strange to see them together on a Saturday, outside of school.

Lumikki had been under the impression they didn't really get along.

"Who would be crazy enough to actually buy something like this?" Aleksi asked.

He was pointing at what had to be intended as a centerpiece: a blinking, red "I Love You" sign.

"Just imagine waking up in the middle of the night to the doorbell ringing and finding something like that sitting outside!" Tinka said, laughing. "I'd be scared out of my mind."

Lumikki shivered.

"I'm starting to think this might not be the best place to do my Christmas shopping," she said, trying to keep her tone light.

"Looking for something for Sampsa?" Tinka asked quickly.

Lumikki nodded.

"Lucky boy. I'm sure you'll find the perfect present for him."

Lumikki thought there was a strangely melancholy shade to Tinka's smile. She didn't have the time or interest to start analyzing that now though.

"Have fun shopping!" Lumikki said and then left before the others could suggest they shop together.

Lumikki left the Stockmann Christmas department and continued down the escalator to the bottom floor.

Maybe she would find something in the book department. The fact that she wasn't seeing anything she thought Sampsa would like was discouraging. Did she really know her boyfriend this poorly? Lumikki didn't want to believe that was the problem. It was just that the whole buy buy buy pressure always made her shut down. It made everything look stupid and tasteless.

Lumikki's hand stroked the covers of the books absentmindedly. None of them seemed to whisper Sampsa's name.

"We have to stop meeting this way."

The hairs on Lumikki's arms instantly stood on end. Blaze was standing next to her.

"This is twice in less than a week. It must be fate. Maybe now I can tempt you with a cup of coffee?"

Lumikki looked into Blaze's laughing eyes and felt herself nodding before she had time to think.

Two hours and four big cups of coffee later, Lumikki wondered where the past year had gone. It felt like she and Blaze had just picked up where they left off. Or maybe not there, exactly, not at the agonizing, final moments of their breakup. A little before, when words still flowed between them naturally and unforced. Now they were sitting at Lumikki's kitchen table again, just like they used to. Drinking coffee. Talking.

"Every day I'm happier and more whole," Blaze said, and Lumikki could see from his direct, placid gaze that he was telling the truth.

Blaze had only told her a little about the details of the sex reassignment process, and Lumikki hadn't asked because she respected Blaze's decision to only share what he felt good sharing. This was about Blaze's body, his own physical essence.

"But I needed all the loneliness and isolation. It helped me go on because it made me strong. I know I hurt you so much, and I want to apologize for that."

There was an honest brightness to Blaze's words. Lumikki still couldn't reply though because she didn't have the words.

Instead, Lumikki told him about everything that had happened over the previous winter and summer: the crimes she had gotten mixed up in, the danger and all the running, how close death had been.

"I read about the thing in Prague in the newspaper. That was crazy," Blaze said, shaking his head.

"I seem to have a habit of getting into dangerous situations," Lumikki tried to joke, but she couldn't force a smile.

Quickly, she tried to cover her anxiety by taking a big gulp of the coffee that was already lukewarm. That always happened to them. They barely noticed as their coffee grew cold, they had so much to say.

But Lumikki didn't tell Blaze about remembering that she used to have a sister. And of course, nothing about the harassing letters, even though she wished she could share the burden with someone.

She couldn't take the risk that this "shadow" would make good on the bloody images he painted in his messages.

Lumikki saw how what she was saying affected Blaze. She saw the desire to protect her that sparked in his eyes. She saw how Blaze's hand inched across the table toward her own, ready to grab it.

"Oh, and I have a boyfriend," Lumikki quickly added.

Blaze pulled his hand back and picked up his coffee cup, feigning nonchalance.

"That's great," he said with a slanted smile.

Lumikki hurried to tell him about all of Sampsa's wonderful qualities. Blaze listened calmly. His expression seemed to say that he didn't consider this boy a particularly important factor in Lumikki's life. Lumikki was a bit offended. Did Blaze really think he could just waltz back into her life after pulling a stunt like disappearing for a year and that Lumikki would accept him with open arms and forget everything?

If he did, he had an infuriating amount of nerve. And he was wrong.

Blaze got up to get a glass of water. When he returned to the table, instead of sitting down, he pressed his hands to Lumikki's shoulders and began massaging them as if that were perfectly natural.

"You're all knotted up," he said.

Lumikki only managed a vague mumble in reply. She knew she should ask Blaze to stop. Theoretically, a shoulder rub was just innocent touching between friends, but they weren't friends. Not only. Not yet. Maybe not ever.

But Lumikki didn't ask Blaze to stop because the rubbing felt so good and her shoulders really were tighter than they had ever been before. Blaze's familiar, deft touch made them relax, and Lumikki could feel her blood flow improving as the clenching in her muscles eased. Blaze's hands were warm and their pressure was both gentle and purposeful. He didn't try to force her muscles into submission. First, he massaged lightly, then gradually pressed harder and deeper. He stopped at the tightest spots and took the time to warm them under his fingers.

Neither of them said anything.

Florence and the Machine played in the background, singing about bruised bodies burning with passionate fire. Lumikki regretted her choice of music. But not really. She had known what she was doing when she put Florence on. She had known what mood it would create.

Blaze's touch made Lumikki slip into a sweet, almost dreamlike state. For a moment, she could forget everything else. The fear. The anxiety. She didn't need to think about anything. The languid relaxation and warmth spread from her shoulders down.

Lumikki didn't know how long had passed when she realized the massage had changed. Now it was more caressing. Blaze gently stroked her neck, and every brush of his hand made shivers run down Lumikki's spine, and beyond. Gradually, the relaxation melted away, replaced by a burning fire. Blaze's hands caressed the sides of her neck and her earlobes, and then returned to the nape of her neck. Warm breath against Lumikki's skin.

The two of them against each other, chest to chest, breath heavy, lips touching.

The two of them in the shower, bare, slick skin, wet, the hard tile wall behind her back, sounds echoing in the small room.

The two of them on Lumikki's bed, the tangled sheets, the panting, the teeth on her shoulder, the cries they couldn't hold back.

The two of them in their own forest, surrounded by the scent of pine, hidden, concealed in the shadows, clinging to each other, lost in each other, and somewhere far away, far above, in the branches, the twinkling light of the stars.

Lumikki snapped out of her daydream. Quickly, she stood up and stepped away from Blaze.

"You need to go now."

Lumikki stared past Blaze with determination. She couldn't take the risk of looking him in the eyes. If she did, she might not have the strength to send him away.

Blaze didn't argue. Calmly, he went to the entryway and dressed in silence for the cold outside. But at the door, he turned and smiled.

"I'll see you again soon, my princess. You know it as well as I do. We can't stay away from each other for long."

Then he left without waiting for Lumikki's reply.

Lumikki stood, staring at the door. She knew that Blaze was right.

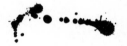

I've seen so often how people can be truly, senselessly cruel to each other. Especially in school. Children and teenagers find each other's vulnerabilities and strike at them without mercy. They are animals. School is a hunting ground and a battlefield. Only the strong survive.

That is really why I dream about getting to carry out my threats. Everyone watching the play. Everyone silent in their seats.

Then the stage fills with shouts and blood and bodies. Panic. The doors are locked. Then it's the audience's turn. One at a time. No one would escape. I would paint the whole theater red.

"Life's but a walking shadow, a poor player that struts and frets his hour upon the stage and then is heard no more: it is a tale told by an idiot, full of sound and fury, signifying nothing."

They would learn that even the strongest, most brutal, and most cunning are not invincible. The laws of life and death are cruel teachers.

SUNDAY, DECEMBER 10

8

Lumikki was jealous. It was the first time in her life she'd realized it this powerfully. She had wanted to be someone else before, of course. Someone who wouldn't need to hide the bruises when she got home and suck blood from her lower lip, to claim that she had just tripped on the way from school. But that had been more of a hopeless desire to get out of her own life than specific jealousy for someone else's.

Sampsa's father carried in a big pile of pancakes and set them on the table.

"These aren't going to win any prizes," he said.

"Well, what do you expect when, the whole time you were cooking them, you had one eye on that iPad game of yours," Sampsa's mother pointed out and patted her husband's arm.

Sampsa's little sister, Saara, was rocking in her chair.

"I'm going to eat at least six pancakes!" she announced.

"How does a penguin make pancakes?" Sampsa asked.

"Um, how?" his sister asked.

"With its flippers!"

"What? Oh . . ." Saara said as the punch line dawned on her and she began laughing infectiously.

"Okay, here's another one," he said. "What dinosaur loves pancakes most?"

"What?" Saara asked.

"Tri-syrup-tops!"

Saara nearly fell on the floor giggling.

"I'm here all week, folks," Sampsa said, looking smug.

"I blame their sense of humor on you," Sampsa's mother said to his father.

Sampsa's dad shrugged, grinning proudly.

Lumikki watched the exchange in bewilderment.

She wasn't used to being in a family like this where people joked and laughed all the time. Sampsa's family also seemed to talk nonstop. Words flew back and forth between them like balls being tossed around, some of them landing on the floor without anyone paying any attention. The conversation seemed almost chaotic, but it wasn't. Everyone more or less kept up. Even Saara, who was only four.

A certain amount of tender chaos characterized other aspects of Sampsa's house as well. Even the most generous person could never have called it tidy. There was stuff all over the place: toys strewn across the floor, clothes draped over chairs, piles of magazines, piles of books, half-opened boxes and packages that could have been coming or going. Lumikki's parents' house never could have looked like that.

Lumikki envied Sampsa's family so much it made her heart ache. Everything showed that their life was here and now. They took care of each other and enjoyed each other's company. They had fun. They were comfortable, without anything contrived or fake or pretend about them, even when a stranger like Lumikki was visiting. They had accepted her like a long-lost relative expected to participate in everything going on. Lumikki had never felt as welcome anywhere as when she stepped over the threshold of Sampsa's home. Her own father's Swedish-Finnish extended family had always felt distant to Lumikki even though they had their own happy songs and liked to talk. Every time she was with them, Lumikki felt like a black sheep everyone wished was different—happier and more social. Sampsa's family was like Sampsa himself: without any demands or expectations.

Out of the corner of her eye, Lumikki watched Sampsa, relaxed and smiling broadly as he piled pancakes onto his little sister's plate. Lumikki knew she could never look like that with her family.

Everything was so good in Sampsa's life. His happiness was self-evident and yet completely deserved. He was a person who had room to be friendly and warm to others. In his world, there weren't any silent secrets or threatening letters or the fear of death. In his world, a girlfriend wasn't supposed to let her ex-boyfriend massage her neck knowing full well the forbidden desire his touch would arouse.

Lumikki watched the bustle of Sampsa's family and suddenly felt chillingly alone. Her fear, her dark places, her anger that ran as red as blood, the black shadows of her forest, her murky waters and deep undercurrents. They would never be these people's life. These happy, sunny, joking, playful, loud, almost irritatingly voluble, and perfectly lovely people's life.

"Now my hands are sticky!" Saara said, holding up red palms.

In the end, she'd only managed to eat three pancakes.

"Well, you did eat half a gallon of strawberry jam on your pancakes. And you ate with your hands."

Sampsa leaned over to wipe his sister's hands with a napkin.

Sticky strawberry jam. Red. Sticky. Warm. Blood.

Images flashed through Lumikki's head so fast she couldn't catch hold of them. In her mind, she saw jam dripping onto the floor. She saw a pool of blood that grew and grew. She shook her head a little. Where were these images coming from?

"Can I go play now?" Saara asked impatiently.

"Yes," her mother replied.

"Lumikki is going to come play princesses with me," Saara declared, grabbing Lumikki's hand with her own still slightly sticky one.

Lumikki flinched at the touch. A bloody hand. A hand that didn't move even when she nudged it. A slowly cooling hand.

"Lumikki might still want to eat. Ask nicely," Sampsa's father said.

"Sure, I'll come," Lumikki said quickly.

She wanted to get her mind away from the strange associations that kept flashing and disappearing like lightning strikes.

Saara put a frilly lace hat on Lumikki's head before pulling a pink dress over her own clothes and waving her magic wand.

"This is a magic wand and a sword at the same time," she explained proudly, showing off the sparkling stick.

"That's handy. If monsters come, you can cast a spell on them and make them nice, or fight them off," Lumikki said.

The lace hat itched on her head, but she let it be. She could stand a little discomfort during the game.

"Monsters are my friends. But if the evil prince comes, I'll chop off his head. And then I'll turn him into a cute little frog."

Lumikki smiled. Apparently, this family had turned the traditional fairy-tale roles on their heads several times over. Saara started dancing wildly in her pink princess dress. Little Briar Rose.

The last letter flashed into Lumikki's mind and she tried to push it back. But it wouldn't go. Its words barged back to the forefront, hitting her like waves rolling against the shore one after another. Ever higher, breaking white.

Briar Rose. Rose.

Lumikki had to sit down on the floor because her legs would have given way. This wasn't a dream or a fumbling fantasy. This was real. This was a memory.

Rose. Rosa.

Her sister's name had been Rosa.

MONDAY, DECEMBER 11

9

Lumikki pressed herself flat against the cold stone wall of the tower room. She stayed perfectly silent and still. First, she became only a shadow, then part of the wall as she melted into it. Lumikki became hard. Her legs and arms froze. Her heart became a rock. Her breath slowed to nothing. She did not exist.

Lumikki knew that the door of the tower room would open, that she would only have a few seconds. She would have to strike instantly. In her hand, she squeezed the silver comb, stroking its sharp teeth with a finger. If she pressed her fingertip against a tooth, it would sink into her skin and make great drops of blood well up. The winding, beautiful ornamental embossing of the comb felt comforting and safe against her hand. It formed an image of intertwining roses.

Briar Rose. Who pricked her finger on a spinning wheel and slept for a century. Rosa, who slept the eternal sleep. Lumikki's sister. No, she couldn't think about that now.

She had to concentrate on when the door would open. All her senses and thoughts had to be harnessed to this.

Lumikki heard footsteps approaching. She could tell from their rhythm it was the person she was waiting for. She hated him so much that her rage nearly blinded her with a jagged haze of red across her vision. Her captor, her oppressor, who had killed the only person Lumikki could imagine loving. Lumikki hated him so much she was ready to kill.

The steps paused at the door. The key turned excruciatingly slowly in the lock. Lumikki squeezed the comb in her hand. As the prince walked in, the opening door concealed Lumikki. The prince looked around at the empty tower room, confused. Lumikki kicked the door shut and attacked the prince. With a single, violent thrust, she plunged the sharp teeth of the comb into the prince's neck. The prince fell, holding his throat.

Blood. Red and warm. The elixir of life pulsing out of the prince with every heartbeat, every leaking drop moving him closer to death.

"Help," the prince beseeched Lumikki as he died.

"Never."

Lumikki stood in the prince's blood and watched as the life began to disappear from his face. She didn't hurry. She enjoyed the moment. *Die, my tormentor. You wanted to lull me into an eternal sleep and close me back up in a glass coffin. You wanted to look at me as if I were nothing more than a beautiful, silent decoration. Not a living person with thoughts and feelings and desires. Difficult to control. My own independent being who doesn't always do exactly what you want.*

"Good, good. Very good. Lumikki, keep that."

Excitedly, Tinka jumped onto the stage and put her hand on Lumikki's arm. Lumikki recoiled. She realized how hard she was breathing. Her hands were shaking and she was almost surprised to find they weren't bloody. She had felt the warm, sticky blood on them. Sticky like strawberry jam. Once again, Lumikki had been somewhere else, so deep in her role that everything had actually been happening to her.

"Is that really believable that she just stands there watching me die? Shouldn't she run away or something?" Aleksi asked, rubbing his neck.

"This is an important climax. Snow White's revenge. Of course she has to stop and watch for a few seconds. The audience has to stop. And this isn't supposed to be realistic."

Tinka sounded irritated again, as she did so often when she spoke to Aleksi.

"Okay, okay. You're the director. It's your vision," Aleksi replied.

Then he leaned over to Lumikki.

"Could you go a little easier with the comb next time? You scratched me pretty bad."

Aleksi showed the red marks on his neck.

"Yeah, sorry."

What Lumikki couldn't say was how surprised she was that Aleksi's neck wasn't spurting real blood. She didn't have any memory of a moment when she could have stopped her attack.

"That's a wrap for tonight," Tinka said and clapped her hands.

Everybody started collecting their things. Sampsa came over to Lumikki and put his arm around her.

"Tonight I'm going to stay over at your place and we can play Snow White and the Huntsman," he whispered into Lumikki's ear.

"The Huntsman dies," Lumikki said with a snort. "I'm not sure I'm really into the necrophilia thing."

"I might rise from the dead with the right encouragement."

Watching their whispering, Tinka's eyes narrowed ever so slightly.

"Let's go before we have to get those two a room."

Aleksi laughed. Lumikki couldn't quite put a finger on Tinka's tone of voice. Maybe there was a little jealousy in it, but was there something else? Something darker? A hard edge under the sarcasm?

In the front lobby, a strange sight awaited them.

Red rose petals had been scattered all over the floor.

"Okay, who's the funny man?" Tinka asked the others.

Everyone just looked at each other and shrugged.

"Nobody else should be here but us," Sampsa pointed out.

"Hello? Anybody here?" Tinka yelled loudly.

Here, here, here, echoed down the empty hallways. No one answered.

"Strange," Aleksi said.

Lumikki looked at the petals and smelled their heady, sickly scent in her nostrils. She knew the roses were meant for her. Her stalker wanted to remind her of Briar Rose. Apparently, he didn't know that Lumikki had already remembered the name. That brought her some degree of satisfaction. Lumikki knew that in at least one area, she was ahead of her stalker.

Once upon a time, there was a key that fit a small chest. Two little girls often played with the chest. It was their treasure chest where they hid jewelry and rocks and bird feathers and perfect pinecones and beautiful autumn leaves and corks and marbles and all the secrets they shared. They were princesses and, when they grew up, they would use the riches in the chest to travel around the world.

Then came the day when the chest was emptied. All of the girls' wonderful treasures disappeared. The chest was filled with other kinds of treasures and secrets. But no one could use them to travel around the world. And besides, one of the girls would never travel anywhere ever again.

Once upon a time, there was a key that had waited long and patiently.

Once upon a time, there was a key that wanted to open the chest again and reveal its secrets.

Once upon a time, there was a key that was moved from its old hiding place to wait in a new hiding place, a cold crevice of rock.

TUESDAY, DECEMBER 12, EARLY MORNING

10

Lumikki woke up hot and anxious. She glanced at her phone. It was 3:20 in the morning. A time she should be happily sleeping the deepest possible sleep. Sampsa's arm was wrapped around her, the boy radiating warmth. Usually that felt good, but right now it was too much heat. Wriggling out from under his arm, she climbed out of bed. Sampsa mumbled in his sleep, but then rolled over and continued his quiet snoring. Happily sleeping away in perfect safety. Lumikki looked at the back of Sampsa's head and his mussed hair, slowly letting herself fill with the tenderness she felt for him.

Sweet, sweet Sampsa. Sleeping like an innocent child. Strangely innocent even when awake. Fearless because he had never really had to fear. Knowing his own worth because no one had ever called his worth into question or trampled it into the ground.

Lumikki closed the door behind her as she went into the kitchen. She turned on the light and tried to decide whether to make coffee. Then she definitely wouldn't be able to get back to sleep, but right now she really needed that strong smell and familiar taste. The sharp bite of the first sip that soon turned to a sensuous feeling of calm and refreshment. Sharpening her senses.

She was just about to grab the espresso pot when she saw her phone display light up. A text message. Who on earth would be texting her at this hour of the morning?

My Lumikki, you're awake. I can see the light in your window. Don't even think about waking up your snoring boyfriend. This is just between the two of us, like all important things.

Lumikki's mouth went dry. It was hard to swallow. Breathing felt difficult. The text message had been sent through an anonymous server, so the phone only displayed the provider's number, not the sender's. Her stalker was leaving nothing to chance, and he hadn't left any traces of himself even by accident. *Escape. Hide. Lights off.*

That was Lumikki's first reaction, but she knew all of that was pointless. She had already been seen. She couldn't hide. So with as steady steps as she could manage, she walked to the window and looked out into the darkness. She forbade her hands from shaking and pressed them against the glass, shading herself a small peephole out into the outside world. There was no one in the park. The shadows of the trees didn't move. But there were too many dark places to count where her stalker could be standing, hidden. Or he could be in the opposite building. He could be standing almost anywhere. He could see Lumikki. Lumikki couldn't see him.

Another text.

Come out. I want to show you something.

Never. Lumikki nearly threw her phone against the wall. Did this person think she lacked any sense of self-preservation? That she was just going to walk out into the night because some lunatic was sending her messages? Lumikki knew she was reckless sometimes, but she wasn't that crazy.

Lumikki sat down at the table and looked at her phone. She could turn it off. Her stalker could send her messages all night if he wanted, but she wasn't going to read any of them.

Just then a third text came through.

I can see you aren't going to come out. Too bad. In that case, I'll have to do something else tonight. I have

Anna-Sofia's address here. I think I'll pay her a visit. Do
you have anything you'd like me to say to her? If you do,
now's the time. In the morning, she won't be able to hear
it anymore. Or anything else.

Lumikki stood up so fast the chair clattered to the
floor. The person sending these messages had to be bluff-
ing. What a bullshit threat. He wasn't going to go kill
Anna-Sofia. He couldn't. He was just trying to see how
far he could push Lumikki.

But what if he was serious . . .

Or did you change your mind? You have two choices,
Lumikki. Either you go outside now or Anna-Sofia dies
before sunrise. Maybe you want her to die. If you do, I'm
happy to oblige. Anything for you, my love.

Lumikki knew she couldn't take the risk. She didn't
know who she was dealing with, but she knew that this
stalker knew things about her he shouldn't have been able
to know. And he really could be prepared to do anything.

Clothes on. Coat on. Boots on. One last careful peek
in to make sure Sampsa was sleeping. Still the same quiet,
peaceful snoring. Lumikki quickly scribbled a note saying she couldn't sleep and had gone out for a walk. She
sincerely hoped Sampsa wouldn't wake up before she got
back. If she got back.

No, Lumikki refused to give in to fear, even though it washed over her in a choking deluge.

Outside, it was drizzling. Before letting the door swing shut, Lumikki squeezed the handle so hard her hand started to hurt. She looked around, but didn't see anyone. What kind of game was this? She had come outside. She was following instructions.

Another text message.

> Good girl. But the night is cold. I want to take you somewhere warm. I know you're a fast runner. You have exactly fifteen minutes to run to Milavida Palace. If you don't make it in time, I'll change my plans and go kill Anna-Sofia after all. Your time starts now.

Lumikki had already set off running as she read the final words of the message. The wet, slick park path seemed to slip away under her combat boots. Why hadn't she known to put on running shoes? She should have learned by now that she always ended up running at some point. That was what her life had been like since last February.

In her mind, Lumikki quickly calculated the fastest route. To the end of the park, across the railroad tracks, and then straight to the river. Gray-brown muck squelched under her shoes. The cold drizzle penetrated her coat and hat, and reduced visibility. The street lamps shone wanly. Everywhere their light didn't reach was as black as pitch.

As she ran and glanced at the time, Lumikki wondered if there was any sense to this. Why was she doing this? Why did she really care whether her stalker carried out his threat? Lumikki hadn't seen Anna-Sofia in more than two years and hadn't had anything to do with her in much longer. It shouldn't have mattered to Lumikki in the slightest what happened to her former school bully.

When Lumikki crossed the tracks and turned north toward the river, she realized this was the only thing she could do because a part of her really did want Anna-Sofia to die. Lumikki had fantasized about it so many times, sometimes even dreaming it would happen. Even after she got away from her tormentors and moved to Tampere, a small part of Lumikki thirsted for revenge and a feeling that evil had received its reward. Because of Anna-Sofia and Vanessa, she had spent years wishing she could be dead instead of having to endure their torture.

Justified revenge.

If Lumikki had just stayed home and gone back to sleep and Anna-Sofia had really died, she would have felt responsible. She would be guilty because a part of her wanted it.

Still five minutes left. Lumikki pounded along the street. She was just coming to the footbridge that led over the river to the park with the palace. The bridge was wet. The cold, damp air was rough on her lungs. But she would make it. She had to make it.

This park wasn't one of Lumikki's favorite places. It was beautiful enough, with a long history since it was built on nearly bare rock back in the early eighteen hundreds. In the summer, it was intoxicatingly green and had amazing views out over the lake. There were all kinds of different rock-dwelling plants, fences built from river stones, and the park even had Finland's biggest poplar tree. Under different conditions, Lumikki would have thought it was the best park in Tampere.

But Blaze had dumped her here. That was why Lumikki could never come here without experiencing a confused mixture of sadness and anxiety. And tonight, the park was black and silent as the grave. A nightmare park.

The palace rose white and woefully run-down in the center of the park, on the highest spot, in stately solitude. Lumikki's lungs hurt as she expended the last of her strength on the uphill sprint.

Milavida. That was the original, melodious name of the place. Milavida's history was tragic. The owner of the Finlayson textile factory, Wilhelm von Nottbeck's son, Peter von Nottbeck, had built it as a replacement for the family's previous house, a villa next to the rocky hill. However, the Nottbeck family never lived in their new house, which was completed in 1898, because Peter's wife, Olga, died giving birth to twins and Peter died six months later after an appendix operation in a Paris hospital. The palace was sold to the City of Tampere in 1905. In the black December night, Milavida looked like the ethereal ghost of a building. A palace of specters. Perhaps the Nottbecks had moved in after all following their deaths.

Lumikki looked at her phone. She had made it in time. She felt like screaming for her stalker to come out and show himself at last. Just then, a new text message arrived.

> One minute early. You were faster than I expected. You've earned your reward. In the foundation of the palace on the left side with your back to the lake is a small hole. There's something for you there.

First, a game of tag and now, hide-and-seek. The stalker must have been getting some sick pleasure from this. Lumikki went to the left end of the building and started feeling along the cold stone foundation with her fingers. Nothing. No hole. She was getting tired of this. Then, just as she was giving up and her fingers were losing all feeling, she found a crack almost at ground level. She pushed her fingers in and caught hold of something metal. Lumikki pulled it out.

In her hand lay a small brass key.

> Congratulations. This is the key to the great secret of your life. I'm sure once you remember enough you'll also remember what the key goes to. But now it's time for

you to go make sure your prince is sleeping safely. You wouldn't want anything bad to happen to him. Even if he isn't your one true love.

Lumikki never would have thought she could run back even faster. Fear gave her wings. If this lunatic did anything to Sampsa . . .

At home, everything was as it should have been. Sampsa was asleep in bed. Lumikki took off her clothes, crumpled up the note about going on a walk and threw it in the trash, and snuck back into bed. In his sleep, Sampsa turned over and hugged her. His bangs were moist. Had he had a nightmare and been sweating?

Suddenly, Lumikki was so tired that her eyes drooped shut. She fell into a sleep free of nightmares or dreams about the mysterious key waiting in her coat pocket. The key with the heart.

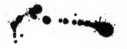

People are so trusting. If you're assertive and credible enough, they swallow your words and love how true they taste. That's why it was so easy to get the key. People trust me and end up saying things they wouldn't otherwise. All I had to do was create a relaxed, confidential mood and even he *talked. And you should never forget that alcohol helps people open up too. The key was hidden where he guessed it would be.*

"Isn't it sick that they still keep it in the bookshelf behind a copy of Tittytumpkin's Fairy Tree?*" That's what he said when I got him drunk. I agreed, although I think there are much sicker things in this world. Who am I to judge other people's decisions? We all want to keep our secrets in our own way.*

I wanted to give it to you so you would remember. I could just tell you everything I know, but that would be boring. I would rather you found it out yourself. Then it will mean more. Then your own, real memories will come back.

You may not be able to think of it this way yet, but I am giving you gifts. One at a time. And these are the biggest gifts anyone has ever given you.

I am giving you your past.

I am giving you your secret.

I am giving you who you really are.

I am giving you yourself. Finally.

And then you will be prepared to accept my final gift, my eternal love, because you will understand that I am the only person who can love you this much. Then you will learn to love me too. We are the same. We are one.

TUESDAY, DECEMBER 12

11

The black water dragged Lumikki ever farther down. She couldn't have reached the surface even if she tried. But she didn't want to try. Under the water was a forest. Different from any forest on land. The trunks and branches of the trees were in a constant, fluid swaying motion. They were flexible. They were soft, water plants.

Lumikki sank deeper and deeper. Now she could see something shining on the bottom. It was a small chest. It looked familiar. Lumikki realized that the brass key she had been given would fit the lock on the chest. They belonged together.

Lumikki tried to get to the chest, but suddenly, her feet became stuck in the black bottom muck. She couldn't move. She couldn't breathe. Her oxygen was running out. Lumikki knew that her lungs would soon fill with water and she would die.

"Fear."

Hearing this word stated emphatically snapped Lumikki awake. She had just nodded off. It took her a few seconds to realize she was in psychology class and that the teacher's voice had woken her up. Running to Milavida Palace the night before felt like a distant nightmare, but two concrete pieces of evidence remained. Insane exhaustion and the small brass key that was in her jeans pocket and kept tempting her hands to finger it over and over again.

The chest. She remembered the chest. But where had she seen it . . . ?

"Fear is one of the primary drivers of human behavior," the teacher, Henrik Virta, continued. "Sometimes I wonder if we should even talk about courage. Perhaps there's no such thing as courage. Only fear."

"How do you justify that?" Tinka asked without raising her hand.

"We often hear that courage is the conquering of fear. As I see it, fear itself is what drives us to act and can make us do things we wouldn't be able to otherwise. So, sometimes, fear looks like courage."

Henrik's voice was deep and pleasant. He had always been one of Lumikki's favorite teachers because he knew how to say things in a way that made you think, but didn't try too hard to be provocative.

"But doesn't fear make you run and courage makes you stay and fight?" Aleksi asked.

"You can think of it that way. But you can also argue that fear gives us instructions about how best to act in any given situation. The fear of death is one of the strongest. And sometimes it makes us run away, but other times, it motivates us to fight," Henrik said.

Lumikki was still tired and would have liked just to lay her head on her arms on her desk and sleep, sleep, sleep. Sitting next to her, Sampsa stroked Lumikki's arm.

"Go home after class and take a nap. You look like the walking dead," he whispered.

"Thanks," Lumikki snorted.

That morning, Sampsa had remarked on how exhausted Lumikki looked. Lumikki had just said that she hadn't been able to sleep very well. What else could she have said? Her stalker was very clear that she wasn't allowed to breathe a word about him or his messages to anyone. Sampsa thought Lumikki should just stay home from school, but she didn't feel like she could stand being alone right now. Rest sounded good right now, though. It sounded imperative.

After class ended, Henrik asked Lumikki to stay after. Sampsa had to hurry to his next class, so he just raised his hand to his ear signaling that he would call. Lumikki nodded in reply.

"I just wanted to check and make sure you're planning to take the psychology college entrance exam in the spring," Henrik said.

"I guess," Lumikki replied.

"I wouldn't ask, but you're definitely the most talented student I've had in years. We aren't really supposed to say things like that, but I wanted you to know."

Henrik patted Lumikki lightly on the shoulder.

"Okay. Thanks," Lumikki said, off balance.

She was relieved when Henrik turned back to his papers, indicating that their conversation was over. Lumikki needed sleep so bad it was painful.

The doorbell woke Lumikki from a dream about kissing Blaze. In her dream, she felt as the brass key slipped from her mouth into his.

Lumikki got out of bed still wrapped in the dream. She peered through the peephole.

Blaze. Of course. Lumikki wasn't even surprised.

She opened the door even though she had promised herself she wasn't going to let Blaze in anymore. The kiss from the dream still tingled on her lips. At first, Blaze didn't say anything. Taking off his orange gloves, he lightly stroked Lumikki's cheek with cool fingers.

"I had to come," he said. "Ever since our last meeting, I've had this feeling you were afraid of something. I had to come make sure you're alright. You know I would protect you from any of the evil in this world."

His words pierced Lumikki like burning arrows. Something inside her cracked and crumbled.

Because someone could see her so clearly. Could sense the emotions she tried so hard to hide.

Lumikki grabbed Blaze by the neck and pulled him to her. She gazed into his eyes as long as she could. Plunging into the ice water. Jumping into the blue of the sky. Stepping into the hottest, blue-white, most incandescent part of the fire. Then she kissed Blaze and let her lips and mouth and tongue communicate all the longing and misery and desire and passion that had been tearing her apart since they broke up.

As soon as the kiss began, Lumikki knew.

This was their forest. This was their lake. This was their ink-black, clear sky full of points of light.

All these things surrounded them simultaneously. Nothing had disappeared. The light finding its tiny paths through the leaves of the trees. The calming dark. The rustling, the scratching, the cooing, the soughing of the wind, the lapping, the gently rocking waves, the cool currents and warm pockets of water, the feeling of weight-lessness, the giddiness, the immensity, time and eternity, the air that flowed into your lungs freely, the pulse of the universe, their shared heart.

Lumikki didn't remember when she had last felt some-thing as hard and unpleasant as breaking away from that kiss. But she had to.

How could something that felt so right be so wrong?

"We can't see each other. At least for a while. I'm with Sampsa now," Lumikki managed to say.

She forced herself to take a step backward. The dis-tance to Blaze felt painfully far. They should have been able to be right against each other. But they couldn't.

"Do you love him?" Blaze asked.

He asked it in such a serious tone that Lumikki felt she owed him an honest answer.

"I'm not sure I know what love is," she said.

"Why are you with him then? Why are you pushing me away? Is it because he's a real boy?"

Exhaustion washed over Lumikki.

"Of course not. Don't even joke about that."

"If I'm not good enough for you, just say so. If I'm too incomplete, too imperfect."

Lumikki heard the hurt and sadness in Blaze's voice, but she couldn't comfort him. Not now.

"This isn't going to go this way," was all she said.

How could she explain to Blaze that everything felt so perfect when she was with him. Everything felt like nothing was missing. But she was with Sampsa now, and Sampsa was nice and sweet and dependable. Sampsa had never broken her heart.

Lumikki knew that if she took one more step into the forest, if she swam two more strokes into the lake, if she let the starry sky descend and fill her soul, she would never get out. She would never want to get out. And she didn't believe she could stand having that all taken away from her again. Blaze had done it once. Blaze had gone and taken the forest and the lake and the stars away. Lumikki couldn't trust that Blaze wouldn't do it again. Lumikki didn't dare allow herself to be hurt again.

"You can't do this to me," Blaze said. "I was only able to make it through all of this because of you. So we could be together again. And now you're turning your back on me."

You turned your back on me, Lumikki thought. *But this isn't revenge. I'm not doing this to you. You're doing this to yourself. I'm punishing myself more than you, denying myself happiness because I'm too afraid. I just can't step into the dark and fall again. I would die. I would go crazy.*

But all she said was, "You went through all of that for yourself, which is how it should be. No one else can make you happy and complete but you."

Lumikki saw Blaze's eyes well up. Their surface quivered, but he just managed to hold back enough to keep the tears from rolling down his cheeks. This suppressed pain hurt Lumikki more than it would have if Blaze had started to cry outright. She had to strain not to wrap her arms around him and hug him long, oh so long.

"You are a cold creature, Lumikki. I thought I knew you."

Lumikki did not reply. She didn't have the words. If Blaze chose to be bitter and hate her, that might make things easier for him. It would be easier for him to break free of her.

When the door slammed shut after Blaze, Lumikki's legs gave out. Collapsing on the entry floor, she sat and felt as the blackness crept from the shadows in the corners over her. It penetrated her ears and nostrils, wriggling down her throat into her lungs and stomach, filling them. Breathing was hard. She was running out of air.

Finally, Lumikki stood up and walked to the kitchen. She needed some strong coffee now. Blacker than the blackness that had made its home in her. As Lumikki measured the coffee into the pot, she heard the mail slot bang.

A familiar fear sank its carnivorous teeth into her neck.

Probably just junk mail, Lumikki told herself.

But instead, a white sheet of paper folded over once sat on the floor. Lumikki shoved open the door and rushed into the stairwell. No one. Not even running steps on the stairs. The elevator was still. Lumikki hesitated for a moment, but then went back inside. She wasn't going to go chasing a shadow. The worst thing might be what would happen if she caught him.

Lumikki didn't want to open the letter, but she couldn't not open it. All it said was:

I love you more than anyone else. Always.

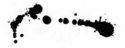

Your touching makes me feel alive. Living feels worth it then.

I've dreamed of you for so long. I've read all the newspaper stories about you. The ones they wrote last summer when you saved those people from the burning building. When I was reading them, I thought that you were a hero, but that the reporters didn't know you. They wrote about you as if you were just a clever or brave girl. They didn't see the fierceness in your eyes.

I know you're like me too. Part of you wanted to watch as the fire consumed that house and those people. You have the element of destruction inside of you. You hide it because our society doesn't approve. But we children of destruction and ruin recognize our kin.

I have dreamed about everything I would do to you if you would give yourself completely to me. All the ways I would touch you. Ways you've never even dreamed of. I know I could make you completely lose control. You would beg me to stop. You would beg me to go on.

Your touch would arouse the beast in me.

But we are both beasts of prey, my Lumikki. We are the ones they try to kill in the fairy tales. We do not die. We always exist in the dark places, behind trees, underground, in deep waters.

The day will come when you are completely mine. That day is coming faster than you know.

WEDNESDAY, DECEMBER 13

12

Lumikki burrowed deeper under the covers. She never wanted to leave this warm nest where momentarily she could be far away from the evil world.

The sleet could lash at the windows. The cold could try to creep through the chinks in the window frames. Under this blanket, she clung to her false sense of security.

Björk was playing in Lumikki's head despite the apartment being silent, singing about playing dead to make the hurting stop. Lumikki imagined an arm around her, warm breath on her neck, a body pressed against her back. She felt it. She felt the hand caressing her shoulder. She felt skin against her skin. She felt the lips that touched her lips and whose kiss made her own mouth open, made her open.

Lumikki felt Blaze. As strongly as if he were really next to her. Lumikki finally understood that this was just the way it was. Blaze lived inside of her even if they were apart. Even if they would never see each other again. Blaze was the one whose hand Lumikki would feel squeezing her hand when she was afraid walking in the dark at night. Blaze was the one whose body heat would radiate into Lumikki when she was sitting in an armchair reading a book. Blaze was the one whose gentle touch would caress her to sleep when she was lying alone. Not Sampsa.

Lumikki felt Sampsa when he was there. When Sampsa was against her. When Sampsa's arms were around her waist and his lips were nuzzling her neck. Then Lumikki didn't feel anything else or think of anyone else. They were just present for each other. But when Sampsa was gone, he was gone. Lumikki didn't feel him next to her like she felt Blaze.

Was that wrong?

Could you live like that?

Lumikki couldn't help her feelings. She couldn't deny them or wish them out of existence. She wasn't going to be able to erase just by force of will the intimacy she felt with Blaze considering that more than a year of separation hadn't done it. The feeling wasn't wrong.

She could decide what her actions would be. She could decide what choices she would make. She had chosen Sampsa. That was just how it was.

Lumikki threw off her blanket and immediately felt the chill. The hard, cold floor brought her body back to reality one toe at a time. She had to venture into the outside world, to school and the hard, piercing gaze of the bright electric lights, which would scare her nightmares away and wipe her skin clean of his touch.

Celestial brilliance, triumphal decree.
Proclaiming the Advent for all to see.
The starry sky burns clear and bright,
Set the candles alight, the candles alight.

The school staircase had been turned into a candle-lined corridor. All the other lights had been shut off. The living dance of the flickering candle flames made the school look like a fairytale castle or nineteenth-century manor house. Lumikki hadn't remembered that this morning was the beginning of the St. Lucia procession. Lately, the tradition had begun spreading from Swedish-speaking circles to Finnish ones as well.

Lumikki always felt conflicted about St. Lucia's Day. There was something warm and safe about it that felt good deep down inside, but there were also unpleasant memories. One year just before she started school,

Lumikki had wanted to play Lucia at home. Her daycare in Riihimäki hadn't adopted the Lucia tradition yet. Her mother had been delighted at the idea and promised to bake Lucia buns and make a white robe and crown of candles for Lumikki to wear. But her father just looked at Lumikki long and hard, his face overshadowed by a grayness that drained all expression away.

"This family is not going to celebrate a woman who tore her own eyes out to stop a man from molesting her because of her beauty. Who was killed by a dagger stuck in her throat after burning her to death didn't work."

Lumikki still remembered her father's words. She remembered how her excitement had died. It was like being forced to swallow icicles whole. Her mother had been furious at her father for saying anything so gruesome to a child. But for Lumikki, it wasn't her father's words that had hurt. The worst thing had been the way he looked right through her as if she and her eagerness and her joy didn't even exist in his eyes.

Lumikki had never suggested celebrating St. Lucia's Day again.

Now she watched as a group of high school girls descended the stairs in long, white dresses, green paper garlands on their heads, tea lights in their hands. Tinka walked at their head. Her long, red hair was an angelic cloud of curls. As she passed Lumikki, she smiled sweetly and squinted a bit in greeting.

When the procession moved on into the mirrored lobby, and their singing began to fade, Lumikki found the words repeating in her mind in Swedish.

Stjärnor som leda oss, vägen att finna,
bli dina klara bloss, fagra prästinna.
Drömmar med vingesus, under oss sia,
tänd dina vita ljus, Sankta Lucia.

Finnish had always been Lumikki's stronger language. She used her Swedish much less frequently. Mostly just with her dad and his relatives. Nevertheless, for her, Swedish was the language of poetry, a language of song that strummed nameless chords of emotion within her.

Drömmar med vingesus.

Vingesus. How could so much beauty fit in one single word? Wings. The rustling of wings. Or soughing, like the song of the wind. Roaring like rapids or the raging of fire. Lumikki heard the word in her ears in melodic tones, sung by the clear voice of a child. The voice was familiar, but it wasn't her own.

Suddenly before her, she saw the steps of an old wooden house with a little girl descending them singing "Sankta Lucia" in Swedish. Rosa. This had to be her lost sister Rosa. She remembered how beautiful Rosa had looked to her, somehow heavenly, and how she had thought that the next year she wanted to be with Rosa singing. Why didn't she have any memory of the following year? Hadn't the next year come?

In her memory, Rosa tenderly smiled at Lumikki. As only an older sister could smile.

The prince laced Lumikki's corset ever tighter.

Just a little more and you will be an obedient wife.

Just a little more and you will learn to behave with more virtue and restraint. You aren't living in the woods anymore. You are a queen. You must walk slowly and with grace. You must hold your tongue when I speak. You may not shout or laugh—that is not appropriate behavior. You have beautiful dresses and precious jewels and gilded chambers. I do not understand why you are not happy. Why can you not be satisfied?

The prince's words echoed in Lumikki's ears. She felt it become harder to breathe. The corset squeezed her lungs shut. The edges of her vision began to quiver and darken.

"Just a little tighter and maybe you'll fall back into your eternal sleep and I can return you to your glass coffin. You were more beautiful to look at there. You were better and easier. I fell in love with the maiden in the glass box, not this unruly, impudent, misbehaving person who is all too normal and real," the prince whispered into Lumikki's ear.

She couldn't breathe.

Her oxygen was running out.

Lumikki tried to gasp for breath. It didn't work. She simply couldn't get air into her lungs. The sensation of drowning. The sensation of passing out. Darkness spreading its wings before her eyes.

Lumikki collapsed, her head thumping on the floor. As her eyes swept across the stage floor, she suddenly remembered where she had seen the chest the key would fit. It was in her parents' bedroom, under the bed, wrapped in a cloth. She had seen it there years ago when she had been in their room getting a thermometer and it had fallen on the floor and rolled under the bed. Lumikki had wondered what the object wrapped in the dark felt could be. Peeking under the fabric, she had seen a wooden chest.

For a fleeting moment, she had thought she remembered something from her childhood about treasures, but then her mom and dad came home and Lumikki bolted from the room like she'd been doing something out of bounds. And she had never asked about the chest. Of course not. She had understood that this secret was none of her business.

But now it was. Because she had the key.

That was Lumikki's final thought before she lost consciousness.

———

Droplets of water on her face. Like a summer rain. Opening her eyes, Lumikki saw Sampsa's worried gaze.

"I'm fine," Lumikki managed to say.

That was a lie, but in a different way than Sampsa would have understood. Lumikki lay on a soft surface, probably a blanket from the props closet, and her feet were elevated. Her corset had been removed. In addition to Sampsa, next to her also stood Aleksi and Tinka, who was holding a water bottle. Apparently, she had been the one sprinkling water on Lumikki's face.

"I said be careful with the corset," Tinka snapped at Aleksi.

"I didn't even make it that tight," Aleksi said in his defense.

"It wasn't because of that," Lumikki said and crawled onto her feet. Her head threatened to go black again, but she refused to give the dizziness power over her. She had to convince the others that everything was okay because otherwise they weren't going to let her leave.

"I probably just didn't eat enough today. And I was up late last night."

Sampsa and Tinka glanced at each other. Aleksi looked relieved. Tinka frowned and looked at Lumikki closely.

"Okay. Stuff like that happens sometimes. And you seem better now," she finally said.

Lumikki hoped no one would notice her legs shaking. Sampsa rubbed her back with safe, calming strokes.

Lumikki felt like leaning against him and letting him support her, but now was not the time for that.

"Let's wrap it up here for today," Tinka said.

"Maybe that's a good idea," Lumikki said. "Since the scene is supposed to end with me getting my laces undone and running off into the forest, we went a little off script."

She'd managed to make the others laugh. Good.

"Dress rehearsal in two days then. And listen, everybody. This play is going to be fantastic! Thank you for all your hard work."

Tinka's energy was enough to get everyone excited. Chattering voices filled the auditorium. Aleksi nudged Lumikki gently on the shoulder.

"Sorry," he whispered.

"Don't worry about it," Lumikki replied.

"And now I'm going to take you home and spoil you rotten," Sampsa whispered in Lumikki's ear.

Lumikki carefully disengaged herself from his embrace.

"That sounds fantastic, but I have to go see my parents tonight."

Lumikki tried to look Sampsa in the eye despite how difficult it was.

"Does it have to be tonight?" Sampsa asked.

"Well, we have this St. Lucia Day tradition in our family." Lie number two. Or, in a way, it wasn't.

Even though her father had said they weren't going to celebrate the holiday, one of his cousins had been organizing parties on St. Lucia Day in Turku for the past few years. Lumikki knew her dad and mom would be there today and wouldn't come home until tomorrow morning. She would have all the time she wanted to inspect the contents of the chest.

Sampsa looked disappointed. Enduring his disappointed and still slightly concerned gaze was hard for Lumikki. But she didn't have any choice. She had to get some answers tonight or she was going to go insane.

As their lips touched, she tried not to think that it was a Judas kiss.

13

Being home without her parents knowing felt wrong. Her footsteps echoed strangely.

The wrong girl in the wrong house, the echoes whispered. *A ghost girl who shouldn't be sneaking around these rooms alone.*

Of course her mom and dad would have given permission if Lumikki had asked, but she hadn't wanted them to know. She didn't want the extra questions that would just lead to more lies. Lumikki didn't want to be the kind of person who lied to her loved ones, but her stalker had forced her into it with his threats.

Lumikki hoped when she finally uncovered the secret, this "Shadow" would leave her alone. What if the stalker was just obsessed with the fact that he knew something Lumikki didn't and the most important thing was exposing the truth?

Lumikki silenced her inner voice that tried to whisper that an all-consuming madness like his was unlikely to be satiated by something so simple.

Her parents' bedroom smelled like it always had. Lavender, fresh sheets, a slight hint of houseplant soil, her dad's aftershave, and the old lace curtains that had been her grandmother's. Lumikki lifted up one corner of the floor-length bedspread and peeked underneath. The blanket she remembered was there on the floor. Lumikki crawled under the bed. It was dusty. Apparently, her dad didn't vacuum as manically now as he used to when Lumikki lived at home. Good for him.

Lumikki lifted the blanket. Suddenly, her heart was pounding frighteningly fast. Her hands were strangely cold and clammy. But all she found under the blanket was a regular cardboard box. Not an ornate chest. A brown cardboard box full of erotic magazines.

Lumikki pushed the box back into place and covered it. It contained secrets, but not the kind of secrets she was looking for. Her parents' sex life was absolutely none of her business and she wished she had never made even this relatively innocent discovery.

She crawled out from under the bed coughing and brushing the dust off the knees of her jeans.

Disappointment. Emptiness. Could she have remembered wrong? Had she just imagined the whole thing about the chest? What if she had just been thinking so hard about having the key that she had invented the memory of the chest and its lock that the key fit in?

No. That couldn't be it. Lumikki wouldn't accept that.

Where in her parents' house would someone hide a chest they didn't want anyone finding?

Lumikki searched the cupboards and closets, the living room, the entryway, the basement, and the small shed in the back yard. No chest. No hint of a chest. Evening had already turned to night. Hope began to change to gray frustration.

Think, think, she urged herself as she sat on the living room couch. Lumikki gently rubbed her temples, trying to ward off an incipient headache. She dug the key out of her pocket and held it in her palm.

Little key in my hand. Tell me where your lock is hid. Lead me to the chest I seek.

The key was just a dead weight in her hand. It didn't have any answers.

"Sometimes what you seek may be closer than you think." Lumikki had always hated "deep" thoughts like that. But now, that was all she heard repeated monotonously in her head. What could be closer than she'd think? Under her butt? Yeah right.

Before Lumikki had even finished thinking her sarcastic retort, she was tearing the cushions off the couch and opening the hide-a-bed.

And finding the chest.

The bed part of the couch was under the cushions, folded in a space you had to pull it out of. Inside the couch, between the bed frame and the floor, was a small space just big enough to fit a flat box for storing sheets and a blanket. But instead, there sat the familiar wooden chest. Lumikki lifted it out with sweaty hands. She didn't waste any time admiring the decorations on the outside. The contents were the important thing. She could barely hold the key. It turned laboriously in the lock. Lumikki had to work to get the lock to finally open.

She didn't know what she had expected. She couldn't say what she believed or hoped she would find in the chest. Suddenly, Lumikki saw before her a childhood she'd never remembered having.

Photographs of a blond, gray-eyed girl who resembled her but not quite. Who resembled her father and mother, but not quite. Rosa Rosa Rosa Rosa. Her sister Rosa. When Lumikki saw the pictures, she suddenly remembered how her sister smelled and how she breathed in her sleep and how her arms hugged Lumikki and sometimes pinched a little too. Rosa's giggly laugh. Her furious tantrums. Her singing and whistling that sounded like a nightingale.

Pictures of two girls together. One was shorter, with brown hair. Lumikki. They sat side by side. They waded in a lake. They ran. They danced under a sprinkler.

Lumikki wasn't looking at the pictures anymore.

All her senses were suddenly awash with memories.

Strawberries in summer. Rosa gave her the biggest, reddest ones. Grandma's attic always smelled of autumn, even in summer. Grandma's old shoes, which were too big for them. They both put one foot in the same shoe. It was impossible to walk without falling. Rosa's hair tangled easily. Lumikki's didn't. Rosa brushed her hair with a hundred strokes and then another hundred. Rain was lashing the window and they built a fort under a blanket that was oranger than orange. When a scary part came in their favorite television show, Rosa put her hands over Lumikki's eyes and whispered that it was only a story. The smell in the rosebushes made her giddy, but the thorns poked them. Adults never understood the best games. Sometimes you had to get the whole floor wet in your room. Because it was the ocean. Rosa's cheeks were salty because she had been crying. Lumikki licked the salt off. She was a cat. They held each other's hands and were never going to be apart. They would always move to the same house and always sleep in the same room. They would be Frog and Toad. They would be Snow White and Rose Red. And if they had bad dreams, they would sleep in the same bed. Warm side by warm side. Breathing in unison. Nightmares could never get in if they slept right against each other.

Lumikki didn't know how long had passed when she finally remembered she was eighteen years old and sitting on the floor of her parents' living room surrounded by photographs. Dozens and dozens of photographs scattered all around. They filled the floor. As if a new sky had opened up above her and colorful, rectangular snowflakes had fallen from it. Lumikki wasn't three anymore. She wasn't holding her older sister Rosa's hand.

Lumikki felt as if a tidal wave had washed over her, stripping away the ceiling, floor, and walls. The floodwater had thrust her into the middle of a black nothingness. There was no safety anywhere, no firm foundation, and everything she had believed was a lie, a black darkness. She had lived her entire life up until now believing that she was an only child, alone.

How could a sister be taken away from a person? How could they have hidden from her the fact that Rosa ever even existed? And why? What had happened to her?

Lumikki stood up. She had to support herself on the edge of the sofa. She felt faint. She felt like vomiting. She felt like crying. Her feet wouldn't carry her weight. She fumbled around on the living room table for her phone. She had to call her mom and dad right now. It didn't matter what time it was. It didn't matter if they might already be sleeping. Liars. Deceivers. You couldn't do things like this to someone you loved. Could you? How could they have concealed something this big from her all her life?

Lumikki had to ask.

Now.

She had to know what had happened to Rosa. Just then, a series of text messages showed up. Lumikki knew immediately who they must be from.

> I see you. You're standing with your phone in your hand. But don't make that call. You don't want the leading role on opening night played by blood spattered on the walls. Blood running across the stage. Enough blood to fill every seat. You don't want your nice but stupid boyfriend falling down in the middle of his lines and staring at you with lifeless eyes. And you know canceling the show wouldn't help anything. I would still find all of you and act out my script. You are beautiful right now. A person who has seen the truth is always beautiful.

Lumikki rushed to turn off the living room lights even though she knew it wouldn't help anything.

Then she stood stock-still in the dark room and stared into the yard, trying to see something. Only blackness gazed back.

Lumikki let the hand holding the phone fall and hang limply. She knew she couldn't call.

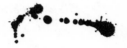

Knowledge is beautiful and cruel, my dear Lumikki. With knowledge, you can do anything. Knowledge leads to action and belief and trust. It gives us true power.

If you know the right people, you can always get more information and find exactly what you're looking for. I know so much about you because I wanted to know. My thirst for knowledge was like a person who has never had a proper drink. I knew how to ask the right questions from the right people. I found ways to get everything everyone was trying to keep secret.

Nothing is secret when you're as thirsty for knowledge as I am.

People are always ready to make an exception once you convince them they have a reason to share. Sometimes that takes money and sometimes other forms of payment. Usually, cash isn't necessary though, because people want to tell what they know, even their most sensitive secrets. It's in the blood.

I've been patiently collecting information about you, piece by piece. I didn't rush. I knew I had time, and when the time was right, you would be ready to accept what I found.

Knowledge is power.

Truth is beauty.

I will make you more powerful and beautiful than anyone else.

THURSDAY, DECEMBER 14

14

Always walk in the light, Lumikki.

Those were Lumikki's grandmother's final words to her. Pancreatic cancer had taken her Grammy five years before. Lumikki had visited Grammy in the hospital and leaned in close so Grammy could stroke Lumikki's cheek with her dry, wrinkled hand. Grammy had been widowed at a young age and left to raise four children on her own. Lumikki had loved Grammy, this strong yet fragile woman, without question or reserve. Grammy had loved her too. Lumikki never doubted that for a second. Her father's parents were more distant, though. They lived in Åland, and Lumikki didn't see them much.

But how could even Grammy have hidden from Lumikki that she had a sister? Lumikki felt as if she had been thrust into a strange, artificial reality where everyone was conspiring against her. Candid camera. A giant play.

A reality TV show that was actually scripted but Lumikki was the only one who didn't know.

Always walk in the light.

Her grandmother's words came to Lumikki's mind as she walked past the central square downtown on her way home from school. The patterns of the Christmas lights bathed the whole street in yellow and gold brilliance. The flower and snowflake shapes, strands of lights wrapped around tree trunks and branches, and the lights and window displays in the stores made you forget that, if the city ever suddenly lost power, people would have to wander in complete and utter darkness. When there was enough light, you forgot the darkness. Lumikki wondered if her Grammy thought that too. That if she just made Lumikki's life full enough of light and joy, the tragedy of the past would disappear.

Because there had to be a tragedy in her past. Lumikki understood that now after seeing the pictures. Only a major tragedy could offer even a partial explanation for the inconceivable fact that her sister had been hidden from her.

Lumikki hadn't slept a minute the previous night. After her stalker's text messages, she had turned off all the lights, closed all the curtains, found the sharpest knife in the kitchen, and curled up in the corner of the couch staring straight ahead. She had listened more carefully than ever in her life and jumped at every howl of the wind, every creak of the house, even the patter of the sleet against the windows. She had been so afraid she thought she might die of it. Lumikki wanted to call Sampsa or Blaze or her parents or the police, but she couldn't.

The stalker had tied her hands and paralyzed her, taking away any room to move or breathe.

As the night slowly dragged on, Lumikki had tried to think who her stalker could be, but she failed to come up with even a remotely plausible answer. A lunatic. A madman. But who could know so much? Who could know about the chest and the pictures and the key? Who could have got their hands on the key? Lumikki's parents, of course, but although she had increasingly begun to doubt their love for her, she still couldn't imagine that they could be behind this kind of harassment. Her own mother and father. No, that wasn't possible.

But Lumikki wasn't really able to give her full attention to the identity of her stalker since she was so consumed by the question of what had happened to Rosa. That felt more important than anything else. She had to get an answer to that before she would be able to think about the rest.

The stalker had given her a key, but still left the larger mystery locked. Lumikki knew she was at his mercy. She was sure her stalker had the answer.

When the December morning had finally cast its tired, gray gaze over the northern hemisphere, Lumikki had crawled off her parents' couch, arms and legs numb, and on the verge of passing out. She took the knife back into the kitchen and then erased every trace that she had been in the house. She completed each motion mechanically. Sometimes you had to run on autopilot when you lacked the strength and resources for anything else.

Just do what you have to. Shut out everything else.

So Lumikki had taken a morning train to Tampere, stopped by her apartment to change and drink a quick cup of coffee, and then walked to school. Normal things, normal life, as if everything was business as usual. All around, people were living their lives, hurrying to work and school. Lumikki felt like she was watching them through glass, from her glass coffin. Present, but not really.

Once upon a time, there was a girl who wasn't.

Rosa, who had just been wiped away. Lumikki, who walked and breathed and must have looked like a perfectly normal living person, even though all she felt inside was blackness. She was just a shell of a person.

At school, the first person Lumikki had encountered was Henrik Virta, her psychology teacher, who looked at her with concern.

"You aren't sick, are you?" he had asked.

"No. Just winter blues," Lumikki had replied.

"At this time of the year, you have to make sure you get enough sleep and light," Henrik had said, smiling warmly.

Lumikki had only had the energy to nod. Next, she had seen Sampsa, who was even more worried about how exhausted she seemed.

"I just stayed up late with my parents," Lumikki had lied. She had started feeling like telling one more lie might make her vomit.

"Crazy Finland-Swede party animals," Sampsa had said with a laugh.

Somehow that had led to the fight. Lumikki was irritated by what Sampsa said and his smile and his tone of voice and, really, everything. It made her mad when Sampsa said he would wait for her in the library after school so they could walk home to her place together.

"I'm so tired all I want to do after school is take my crazy Finland-Swedish nap alone in my crazy Finland-Swedish apartment," Lumikki had said.

"I promise to be quiet and not bother you," Sampsa had replied calmly.

"No. I want to be alone today."

"You want to be alone a lot lately."

"That's just how I am. You knew that when you started dating me."

"Sometimes I feel like I'm a pretty insignificant part of your life."

Lumikki had seen the sadness in Sampsa's gaze and, under different circumstances, it would have hurt her. But not today. She was so tired and anxious and felt so weighed down that Sampsa's sorrow only felt accusatory.

What could Lumikki have said?

I don't want you with me because every word I say to you is a lie? I'm lying to you to protect you, but today I can't do it anymore? You can't save me. No one can.

She had gone through the whole school day in an impenetrable black fog. Now she was crossing the bridge over the river rapids in the center of the city with an honor guard of horses made of light. Lumikki had always thought this was the best part of the city's Christmas lights. Rearing horses with front hooves pawing the air, their proud neighing almost audible.

Always walk in the light.

She would never get out of the blackness until she knew.

Lumikki decided that it was time to contact her stalker herself for the first time. Pulling her phone out of her pocket, she sent a text message to the number service the stalker was using.

I want to meet you.

Lumikki hoped that would be a strong enough invitation for her shadow. If she had gleaned anything about her stalker's mind, she believed he wouldn't be able to resist the temptation.

Lumikki knew she was playing a dangerous game, but she had to find out who was behind this.

A surprise was waiting for Lumikki at her door. Sampsa. He was sitting on the stairs with a picnic basket next to him.

"If you want, I'll leave. But I thought it might do you good to have a little food and maybe a neck rub."

Sampsa looked so disarming and sweet in his big, light-green hat with his eyes full of hope that Lumikki thought her heart would break. What had she done to deserve such unselfish, unshakeable love?

"Did you really think you were going to take me on a picnic in December?" Lumikki asked.

"Of course. I have a blanket and everything. Your apartment is small, but there's plenty of space on the floor."

Sampsa grinned. Grabbing the boy's coat collar, Lumikki kissed him long and tenderly, because right now Sampsa deserved that more than anyone else in the world.

Inside, Sampsa really did spread the blanket out on the floor and then proceeded to produce baguettes, fresh cheeses, grapes, and chocolate muffins. He put on an album of modern folk songs. Sampsa sat Lumikki down, offered her bread with cheese, poured her a glass of red wine, and put his hands on her shoulders.

"Now you just enjoy," he whispered in Lumikki's ear. Lumikki closed her eyes. Sampsa was so good and so nice that Lumikki was afraid she would burst into tears.

The rhythm and words of the soothing song, Sampsa's warm touch, the warmth of the red wine in her veins. All of it together formed a soft, fluffy, fairy-tale world around Lumikki. What if she could just stay here? What if she could just forget everything else? Just for a few moments?

Sampsa's massage was pleasant. But Lumikki still couldn't help thinking of the other hands that made her skin feel electric in an entirely different way, sending shocks of pleasure through her whole body with only a few light strokes. Blaze. She thought of Blaze even though Blaze was precisely the one she shouldn't have thought about. That wasn't fair to Sampsa.

Just then, Lumikki's phone dinged with a text message. She reached for it.

"Don't look at it now," Sampsa begged.

"I have to," Lumikki replied and grabbed the phone.

Sampsa's hands slid off her shoulders. The fluffy clouds had dissipated already anyway, and Lumikki's heart was pounding in her ears, equally from horror and hope. But the text message wasn't from the stalker. It was from Blaze.

I think about you all the time. First thing in the morning and last thing at night. And all the time in between. I still love you. I will always love you.

Lumikki felt her cheeks flush. Could they really have such a strong connection that when she thought of Blaze, he sensed it? Lumikki stood up. She walked into the kitchen.

"Who was it from?" Sampsa asked.

"My mom. I accidentally left a shirt at their house." Lie, lie, lie, lie. Another lie.

Automatically, Lumikki had opened the kitchen drawer where she kept the dragon brooch Blaze had given her and picked it up. Her fingers stroked the intricate scales. Oh, if only Lumikki could have pinned it to the collar of her coat and worn it proudly. Why couldn't her life be that simple?

Lumikki heard Sampsa get up from the blanket. She quickly slipped the brooch into her pocket. Then she deleted the text message from Blaze. What she really should have done was delete his number from her phone entirely. Lumikki couldn't do that yet though.

Lumikki listened to the words in the chant that was playing—the singer had such an alluring voice, but the meaning was so sad.

"Can we turn the music off?" she asked Sampsa.

"Of course. What do you want to do?"

"Sleep," Lumikki replied without looking Sampsa in the eyes as she walked to the bed.

Suddenly, she was so tired she couldn't stay upright. Lumikki threw herself on the bed with her clothes on, wrapped a blanket around herself, and fell asleep instantly.

Lumikki wasn't immediately sure what had woken her up. She glanced next to her. Sampsa was sound asleep. Lumikki leaned up on her elbows and looked around. Sampsa had cleaned up the picnic and folded the blanket. Lumikki had been sleeping so deeply that she hadn't heard a thing.

Not until she looked at her phone to check the time did she realize a text message had woken her. It was 10:15 p.m. This time, the message was from the stalker.

Come to Särkänniemi. What better place than an amusement park for us to meet? I'll tell you everything there.

Often, I watch you even when I can't actually see you. I have a special place just for that. I have pictures of you. I took them secretly. In the pictures, you are so sweet and contemplative since you thought no one could see you. I hung the pictures on the walls of my secret room. Sometimes I stroke your forehead with a finger. I touch the curve of your full lower lip and think about what it would be like to kiss you.

I also have all the newspaper articles about you. And a lot of files you don't even know exist yet. I made a timeline of your life on one wall. So much has happened to you.

Did you think you lost that orange mitten of yours? I have it. That and your silver pen and the button that fell off

135

your white blouse. They are the small treasures I caress since I can't caress you yet.

Sometimes I come to my "Lumikki room" with candles and talk to you. I watch as the glow of the flames makes your cheeks redden in the photographs. You are so beautiful. You are the most beautiful thing I know.

Pictures aren't enough, though. Mementos are just substitutes.

I want you completely, with all my senses. I want to see you, to smell you, to taste you, to touch you. I have never wanted anything or anyone this much. You are the purpose of my life and the meaning for my existence, my dear Lumikki.

15

Lumikki climbed over the fence of the amusement park, hoping she wasn't going to trip some sort of alarm. The temperature had dropped below freezing and the fence was slick. However, she managed to get to the other side without any sirens going off. Frost glittered on everything like a layer of magic dust. The otherwise empty, quiet amusement park looked eerie and threatening. The dark rides rose into the night like sleeping monsters with many arms. They were motionless, but appeared as if at any moment they could tear themselves loose of the ground and start walking. The swing carousel could have begun spinning wildly and the chains of the chairs could have snapped, sending them flying in every direction. The

Magic Carpet could have taken flight and landed in the lake, sinking gurgling under the waves.

The rides had been left to hibernate for the winter. There was no call to wake them because they would be angry.

Lumikki had managed to slip away again without Sampsa waking up. The boy had a gift for deep sleep. This time, Lumikki had left so quickly that she hadn't even left a note. She couldn't risk him waking up. Lumikki had to meet this "Shadow." She had to get answers.

Now she was inside the amusement park, but she saw no sign of the stalker. Lumikki was tired of all this hiding.

"I'm here!" she yelled as loud as her lungs would allow.

The echo reverberated off the walls of the rides. No one answered.

Come to the fun house.

A text message again. Why was this jerk still running her around? She had already come here, put herself in danger. She was ready to meet.

The door to the fun house was open. Lumikki called inside. There was no reply. She stepped in. A tilting floor, a rope bridge, a ball pit, and a hall of mirrors that made you look tall or short, fat or as thin as a rail. Lumikki had been here before. She could run through it quickly. Even the blackout hall and the glass labyrinth. And the slides at the end.

Next text message.

> Good. Now you've been through the strange stage we call childhood. It is skewed and distorted. You can't always trust your memories. Mirrors lie. Now it's time for you to move on to the Tornado.

Lumikki was growing frustrated and losing hope. She wanted to put an end to this. But maybe it really was the last leg of her journey. Maybe she would get her answers once she had completed these tasks.

The Tornado was the park's wildest ride, a roller coaster with crazy corkscrews. Riders sped along, suspended beneath the track, sometimes upside down. The Tornado also had an enormous loop that swung all the way around.

Next instruction.

> Climb along the track.

This guy had to be completely out of his mind. Only a crazy person would go climbing on a roller coaster track. But this time, the crazy person was Lumikki, because she did as she was told.

Climbing along the icy track was difficult. The metal surface was slick, making it hard to get a grip. Lumikki managed to crawl along the first few yards of flat track, but as soon as the slope increased, climbing became almost impossible. Lumikki's strength was almost gone already. She crept along the track on her hands and knees, hanging when it twisted and turned sharply, holding on with her legs in a vise grip. Sometimes, she pulled herself up with only her arms. Lumikki clenched her teeth, unwilling to give in. She made the mistake of looking down. She was high up. Too high up. How high did the stalker want her to go? Lumikki closed her eyes and tried to breathe. The frigid wind lashed her cheeks. This was crazy. She could fall and die at any second. Suddenly, someone yelled from below.

"Lumikki!"

Lumikki would have recognized that voice anywhere. But she couldn't believe her ears. She glanced down again. Yes, she had heard right. Blaze.

"Come down from there! Carefully!"

Suddenly, Lumikki had lost all feeling in her arms, her legs, her cheeks, and her heart. *Blaze.* The person she loved most in all the world. The person she trusted most in all the world, despite it all. Was Blaze . . . ? Could he be . . . ? Lumikki couldn't think the thought through to its logical conclusion. But what other explanation could there be?

But then she heard another voice. Almost as familiar.

"What the hell are you doing? Come down before I call the fire department!"

Sampsa.

Lumikki didn't understand anything anymore. How could Sampsa and Blaze both be here? Her strength flagged even more. Lumikki decided to start climbing down. It was even more difficult than climbing up. The metal surface tried to slip out of her hands. Lumikki wrapped her legs around the edge of the track, but they slipped too. She ended up hanging by her arms.

Lumikki felt her grip failing.

But Sampsa and Blaze managed to catch her. For a moment, Lumikki was in both of their embraces, both sets of arms protectively encircling her. Protecting or imprisoning. Lumikki didn't know which anymore. She extracted herself from their arms and took a few steps back.

"What the hell are you two doing here?" she asked.

"We could ask you the same thing," Blaze replied confrontationally.

"I asked first, so you answer first." Lumikki did not avoid Blaze's gaze.

Blaze looked away first.

"Okay. I was hanging around outside your apartment because I couldn't sleep. I guess I was hoping I might catch a glimpse of you or something, maybe in the window," Blaze admitted. "And when I saw you go out, I decided to follow you."

He sounded sincere. But Lumikki wasn't sure whether she could trust anyone anymore. She shifted her gaze to Sampsa.

"And you?"

"I read the text you got. It didn't wake you up right away. And when you woke up, I pretended to be asleep and then followed you. For a while now, I've been feeling like you must be seeing someone else."

At first, Sampsa looked ashamed, but then he raised his jaw defiantly.

"And apparently, I was right. You came here to meet him."

Sampsa emphasized the last word with disdain and nodded toward Blaze.

"No, I didn't," Lumikki said.

"Well then why did you come?"

Lumikki didn't answer. She was so confused. Was Blaze telling the truth? Was Sampsa telling the truth? Wasn't either of them the stalker? Or could they both be together? Was this another conspiracy?

"Whatever happened, it's pretty clear you aren't needed here anymore," Blaze said to Sampsa.

Turning to Blaze, Sampsa stepped too close to him, invading his personal space.

"I'd like to remind you that Lumikki is my girlfriend," Sampsa said.

"Who kissed me only a couple of days ago."

Sampsa looked to Lumikki as if asking her to deny this.

Again, Lumikki didn't reply, but her eyes said enough. Sampsa shoved Blaze.

"Get out of our life!" he snapped. "You already left her once. You missed your chance."

Blaze gave a crooked smile and pushed Sampsa back gently, almost playfully.

"True love doesn't care about things like that. Lumikki and I belong together. It's fate."

"You talk pretty big considering you weren't man enough to stand by Lumikki's side," Sampsa spat.

"Oh, so now we're going to see who the real man is?"

Suddenly, Blaze and Sampsa were wrestling each other. Both growled curses even as they shouted at each other that Lumikki really loved them. Dead tired, Lumikki watched the display, once again as if through glass. She didn't cheer either on or wish that either would lose. The fight just looked stupid. Juvenile.

"I can't handle this right now," Lumikki sighed. "You two can stay here and beat each other to a bloody pulp for all I care. I'm leaving. And don't bother following me."

Then Lumikki took off running without a backward glance. She wanted to feel her exhausted muscles strained even further. She wanted the frozen air to torture her lungs. Lumikki wanted something, anything that would clear the fog of uncertainty from her mind.

Could a person go crazy without knowing it? Or was that the normal way of going crazy? What if she really had lost her grip on reality, if she had just imagined it all? What if the letters had never existed? Or the text messages? Or the stalker?

What if it had all just been in Lumikki's head?

Lumikki jumped against the fence, grabbed it with her fingers and the tips of her shoes, and climbed over. She continued running. As she reached the main road that ran along the shore of the lake, someone shouted after her.

"Hey, baby! The party's just getting started!"

A group of middle-aged men, apparently just leaving a Christmas party at the marina. Their elf hats and red noses suggested as much, anyway. Lumikki just kept on running. She would have liked to run away from everything, away from her life, away from the madness that her days had turned into.

She still didn't have any answers. She still didn't know who was stalking her.

When Lumikki opened her apartment door, she felt like collapsing on the floor and crying. How much could a person endure? How much did she have to carry on her own? Where was the point after which a person just broke?

Lumikki was in such a state of confusion and distress that she realized too late there was a smell that didn't belong. By the time she noticed, her hands were already twisted behind her back in a tight grip, a leather glove was shoved in her mouth, and her sleeve was pulled up.

Lumikki's last awareness was of the sharp point of a needle pressing against her bare arm and something being injected into her vein.

Then the world was replaced by blackness.

FRIDAY, DECEMBER 15, EARLY MORNING

16

The shadow hovered sometimes closer and sometimes farther off. Its silhouette was indistinct and shifting. She couldn't quite make out its shape.

Lumikki tried to focus. Everything was so blurry. Her head ached and her arms and legs felt heavy like in a nightmare. Her eyelids wanted desperately to fall back shut. She forced them open.

Lumikki was lying on her back. She moved her left hand away from her body and it struck an obstacle. The same thing happened with her right. And both legs. She managed to lift one of her hands up far enough to discover a barrier there too. Strange. She could still see up and to the sides. Or she would have been able to if everything weren't so cloudy. Cloudy eyes, cloudy thoughts, neither of which she could seem to focus.

"And it wasn't long before she opened her eyes."

The voice came from above Lumikki. It came from the shadow that moved. Lumikki had the vague realization that the voice was familiar, but she couldn't put her finger on it.

"I knew you would be stronger than the princess in the story. No poison could affect you for very long. You're a fighter. You've been fighting your entire life. You've fought against me valiantly too. You didn't show your fear. You didn't tell anyone."

The fog began to clear a little from Lumikki's head. Finally, she realized what was blocking the slow, labored movements of her arms and legs. She was in a casket. In the glass coffin from the play.

"But now your struggle is over," the shadow's voice continued. "You don't have to fight anymore. You can give in now and be mine."

Lumikki tried to sit up. She felt as if her veins had been poured full of black lead. Her head banged against the glass top of the coffin. She struggled, managed to lift up her hands, and tried to push the cover off.

It should have been easy. She knew that. She had done it time and time again in rehearsal. Now the cover didn't budge.

"Poor little Lumikki. Sometimes life surprises us. Everything doesn't go the way we thought. Sometimes you can't get out of a glass coffin so easily. You see, this isn't a play. This isn't a fairy tale. This is real. And in reality, of course, the coffin's lid is screwed shut."

Lumikki tried to make her fumbling mind recognize the voice. It was so familiar. She should have known. She should have been able to think of the name.

The name was so familiar.

She had said it so many times.

She just couldn't find it in the haze that shrouded her brain. But she knew the voice wasn't lying now. The lid really was screwed shut.

"What may surprise you to learn is that a glass coffin screwed shut is completely airtight. So you should be saving your breath. The oxygen won't last forever. And I'm sure you'd rather stay conscious while I'm telling you everything I know about you."

Lumikki lay back down. *Relax*, she ordered herself. *Only breathe as much as you have to. Stay calm. Otherwise you're never going to survive this.*

You're never going to survive this.

Terror crept along Lumikki's neck as she heard the words echo in her mind. They could easily be true.

"I'm sure you've read all of my letters, so you're well acquainted with how much I know about you. I've been studying you for quite some time. I've followed you and watched you, guarded you and protected you, spied on you and followed your steps. I've done this because when I met you, a feeling came to me that you and I are the same. There is a darkness that lives in us."

Lumikki felt like vomiting. She wasn't sure whether the nausea was a result of the words or whatever he'd drugged her with. She tried to breathe more evenly. To bring her heart rate closer to resting.

"You may have balked at all my talk of blood and killing. I've seen your expressions once or twice when you were reading my letters. You looked shocked and afraid. Needlessly. I never would have written those things to you if I didn't know you are a killer too. Actually, of the two of us, only you are a killer. I just enjoy the idea of killing. I suppose it's unavoidable that eventually I'll carry out my fantasy. That hasn't happened yet though. If you had been stupider and told someone about my letters and messages, I would have carried out my threats. It would have given me a reason and a justification. What is your reason and justification, my love? Just the desire to kill? An innate evil? Not to worry, though. Either option is just as stimulating for me."

The shadow circled the glass coffin like a predator his prey. Considering how to strike and at what opening. Would he sink his teeth first into the thigh or the arm or the throat?

"I don't know whether you're just a good actor or if you really don't remember. I suppose that your memories must have begun coming back when you read my letters. Your bloody hands. How you killed your sister, Rosa."

Lumikki's pulse shot up to panic levels. Could this shadow really know something like that? Could it be true? Had she really killed her sister?

"Oh my dear Lumikki, how pale you look. Perhaps you didn't remember. How you plunged the sharp knife into your sister's stomach and stood coldly watching as she bled out. You didn't call the babysitter to help. By the time she arrived, it was already too late. I've read all of the police reports."

Lumikki's clouded thoughts and senses completely lost their hold on the present, but the shadow's words suddenly made the past snap into focus. Closing her eyes, she was three years old.

Lumikki was three and Rosa was six. Mom and Dad were away somewhere, probably at the theater, and their baby-sitter was a bored teenage girl from next door, Jennika. That night, Jennika and her boyfriend were having a fight, which she was thrashing out on the phone, repeatedly calling the boy, her own friends, and the boy's friends. All Lumikki and Rosa got to eat for dinner was some barely reheated leftover pancakes and strawberry jam.

"So why do you get to suck face with whoever you want but I'm a whore if I just talk to a guy?" Jennika snapped angrily into the phone.

"What's a whore?" Lumikki asked.

"It's a girl with lots of boyfriends," Rosa replied with the assurance of a wise older sister.

Jennika glanced at them wearily.

"Take care of your sister," Jennika told Rosa, pointing at Lumikki. "Try not to kill each other for a few minutes."

Then Jennika went upstairs so she could talk in peace.

There was too much strawberry jam for the small pancakes, so the plates were covered with the excess.

"Let's play death!" Rosa suggested.

"How do we play that?" Lumikki asked.

"Like this," Rosa explained and rubbed strawberry jam on the front of her white nightshirt. "This is blood."

Lumikki did the same. The jam was slippery and it dripped on the floor. Her hands got sticky. Lumikki laughed. Rosa wasn't satisfied, though.

"There has to be a weapon for blood to come out," she said, walking to a drawer.

Lumikki was startled to see a knife in Rosa's hand.

"We're not allowed to touch the knives," she whispered.

"Mom and Dad aren't here. And besides, this is just a game," Rosa said.

"Okay," Lumikki whispered uncertainly.

"I'm so sad. I just want to die," Rosa explained.

"Why?"

"Maybe my boyfriend just left me. And now I don't want to live anymore!" Rosa lamented in a dramatic voice, waving the knife in the air. "I'm going to kill myself!" Then she pointed the tip of the knife toward her stomach. In the air, of course, a safe distance from her nightshirt.

Everything happened quickly. Rosa slipped on the jam on the floor. She fell forward, holding the knife, which sank into her stomach. Collapsing on her face on the floor, she didn't get up. Lumikki ran to her sister's side and nudge her shoulder. Rosa did not react. Blood began pooling under her.

"This is a stupid game," Lumikki said. Rosa didn't answer.

"Talk to me!" Lumikki demanded, shoving Rosa over on her back with all her strength.

Her sister's eyes were open, but they weren't looking at Lumikki. Blood trickled from her mouth.

Lumikki realized that something was very wrong.

She ran and ran and ran upstairs. She screamed for Jennika. Jennika was in the bathroom. She was crying and yelling.

"I've never loved anyone as much as I love you!"

Lumikki pounded on the bathroom door.

"What is it now?" Jennika snapped through the door.

"Rosa. Rosa. It's a stupid game."

"Well, tell her you want to play something else. Leave me alone for a few seconds now, will you?" Jennika said in a tearful voice.

Lumikki was crying too, but no tears were coming out.

She ran to the medicine cabinet in her parents' bedroom and took out a package of Band-Aids. If you're bleeding, you need a Band-Aid. She grabbed the ones with Mickey Mouse on them. Rosa liked those.

Then she ran back downstairs. Rosa was still lying on the floor. There was so much red blood. The knife was sticking out of her stomach. It looked wrong. A knife wasn't supposed to be like that. Lumikki tried to take it out, but she failed. She put Band-Aids around the knife, but they were instantly soaked with blood. Rosa's white nightshirt was all bloody. The Band-Aids didn't help. The owie didn't go away.

The blood was slick like strawberry jam, but it was warm, not cold.

Finally, a red-eyed Jennika came down sniffling. She stopped in the doorway to the kitchen.

"Oh my God . . ."

"We were playing death," Lumikki said. "But it's a stupid game. I don't like it."

Lumikki knew the memory was true. She hadn't imagined it and it wasn't a result of the drugs. That was how it had all happened. And the memory explained every one of the strange flashes and nightmares Lumikki had ever had. She had a sister who had died. But it had been an accident. She wasn't a killer.

Did her mom and dad think she was? Did they think that Lumikki had taken the knife out of the drawer and stabbed Rosa in the stomach? Was that why they had hidden her sister and everything that happened? Lumikki had to talk to them. Right now. She had to get out of this stupid glass coffin.

Carefully, Lumikki tested whether the weakness and heaviness in her arms and legs had faded at all. It hadn't. Breathing felt more arduous now too. Her oxygen was running out.

"Everyone thought you were so small you couldn't understand what you did. They considered it an accident. Things like that happen sometimes when normal children are playing. But what normal child wouldn't have immediately run to get the babysitter? And according to the child psychologist, you were uncommunicative, even angry. You kept repeating how stupid Rosa was. When I read your files, I saw deep into your soul. I saw that it is just as black as mine. As black as ebony. And that was when I began to fall in love with you."

No, no, no.

Lumikki shook her head. It didn't happen like that. Jennika lied. She remembered being surprised about it even then. She had hated Jennika for lying, and she had hated her mother and father for being away from home, and she had hated Rosa who had wanted to play a game that turned out real. She had hated her sister because she died. She had hated Rosa because she had loved her so much and because, suddenly, she was gone.

Lumikki tried to breathe more sparingly. She was beginning to feel the lack of oxygen as an increasing faintness and blurring of her eyes.

Was this glass coffin going to turn into her actual coffin?

Lumikki searched her clothing for anything she could use as a weapon to get out. She didn't have a belt with a buckle to use. Not even a hairpin. One hand groped in her trouser pocket. Something metal. Something cold. Something whose surface felt very familiar against her fingers. Her own personal dragon.

It was a brooch, and brooches have pins. What if Lumikki could scratch the glass with the pin and weaken it? She squeezed her fingers around the dragon. She searched for the clasp and opened it. The pin was sharp. Slowly and carefully, she brought her hand out of her pocked. The shadow was on the right side of the glass coffin now. Lumikki pressed the pin against the left wall of the coffin as hard as she could and scraped it down the glass.

The thin pin gave out instantly, bending beyond any use.

Tears of fear and frustration welled in Lumikki's eyes. She was never getting out of this coffin.

Perhaps you're wondering why you.

Because you are special, my dear Lumikki. There is light and darkness inside of you. You aren't like all the others. You're stronger than anyone else I've seen, even though you're also so fragile and vulnerable. You aren't afraid to be alone. You know that the others aren't quite as valuable as you. There are so many facets and layers to you. You have depth at eighteen most other people will never have.

You have experienced sorrow and hate. You aren't only good.

I knew that we would meet as equals because the same black blood runs through us. That's something no one else can understand.

When I saw you for the first time, I knew instantly. It's been years since then. You didn't know then how deeply and truly I saw you. Someone had just left me, someone who had never been able to value my ideas and my deepest inner self. After she left, I thought I might never find someone like me.

Then you came.

You came like a quiet storm. The others didn't understand your power, but I felt the wind and saw the thunderclouds and the lightning and all the magnificence and beauty that only exists in the most violent storms. Riders on the storm.

That's what we are. Riders on the storm. The laws and norms of this world and society don't apply to us because we are exceptional creatures.

I'm so happy that you will soon be mine. Only mine.

17

Lumikki felt as if her heart would stop when Florence and the Machine's "Breath of Life" began echoing in the auditorium.

"This is your favorite, isn't it? Don't look so surprised, my dear. I told you I've been following your each and every step. I know what music you listen to. And I thought this would be a good fit for the occasion. You're longing for a breath of air to save you. You need oxygen. You'll get it soon. I just have to ensure first that you really love me too and understand that we have to be together, the two of us."

The shadow's voice had grown tenser. Lumikki's brain still couldn't quite get a grip on it. She couldn't put it in the right box and attach the right nametag to it.

What was this lunatic? And what did he intend to do to Lumikki?

Lumikki knew that she couldn't just wait and see. She had to do something.

Lumikki could still feel the scales of the dragon against her fingers. Holding the pendant comforted her even though the pin was bent. She stroked the surface of the skin with her finger—its head and ears, the wings lying along its back, the tail that ended in a sharp point. So sharp that it hurt Lumikki's finger.

The tip of the tail. It was clearly stronger, more substantial than the pin.

Lumikki calmed her racing pulse. She had to stay calm. The harder her heart pounded, the more oxygen she would need. And she was out of that. Hypoxia. Oxygen deprivation. Lumikki refused to think about what would follow and how quickly.

She furtively pressed the tail of the dragon against the glass, strained with all her might, and pulled. She felt the metal bite into the glass. The dragon would leave a mark. How deep? Would it weaken the glass enough?

Lumikki knew that she would only have one chance. She had to succeed on the first try.

The pendant left a scratch. Lumikki's hand trembled as she slipped the dragon back in her pocket. For a moment, she collected all her strength. She had to hold on. Her oxygen had to last a few more seconds.

Lumikki filled her lungs with all the oxygen she could still get inside the coffin. Then she slammed her elbow with all her strength right into the scratch she had made. Such intense pain shot through Lumikki's elbow that her vision flashed red.

But the glass shattered. The wall of the coffin collapsed, and Lumikki rolled out, shielding her face. The sharp, jagged glass tore at her clothing and arms. Tiny shards of glass penetrated her skin. Lumikki didn't care.

The shadow was at her side in a second. Lumikki had expected as much.

"I should have guessed you wouldn't wait patiently . . ." he said, bending over her.

Again with her elbow, Lumikki hit him straight in the nose and when the shadow stood up howling in pain, Lumikki succeeded in lifting herself up enough to strike the shadow in the crotch with her other elbow.

It worked. The stalker bent over double.

Lumikki rolled to the edge of the stage and off. She tried to fall as softly as possible, but the hard floor hurt. Her legs still felt like two heavy bars of lead. She knew she

SALLA SIMUKKA

wouldn't be able to stand. Not yet, at least. She started dragging herself across the floor with her arms.

She had to hide somewhere quick. Hide. But where?

Her Finnish classroom was next to the auditorium. Lumikki began hauling herself that way. She covered the distance with painful slowness. Her elbows hurt. The glass shards felt like they were digging deeper into her skin.

Somewhere behind her, the shadow groaned. He would recover from her blows soon enough. Catching up would take him no time at all.

The door to the classroom was open a crack. Lumikki could already hear the shadow moving. Lumikki pushed the door open, dragged herself inside, and managed to lever herself up high enough to grab the handle and push the door shut. Immediately, she felt the shadow tugging at the door handle from the other side. Lumikki clenched her teeth together in pain and, with other hand, stretched up to turn the lock.

Then her strength gave out and she collapsed with her back against the door, panting.

"Oh Lumikki. My poor little Lumikki," the shadow laughed through the door. "Do you really think I don't have a key? Of course I do. You just wait here while I get it from the locker room. Then we can chat some more."

Lumikki felt like she couldn't breathe all over again.

18

The fear of death was a wondrous thing. The survival instinct pumped Lumikki's muscles full of strength they didn't otherwise have. Suddenly, Lumikki's arms and legs worked again. Her brain issued commands to her muscles so quickly that she didn't have time to clothe her strategy in thought. She just acted.

As many desks and chairs in front of the door as possible. Those would slow him down. Collect everything loose she could throw. Open the window.

Already the key turned in the lock.

"Help!" Lumikki shouted out the window as loud as her lungs could manage.

She didn't see anyone outside. But there had to be someone in the park, a dog walker or someone on their way downtown or to the library?

The door slowly opened a crack. The legs of the desks and chairs screeched on the floor as they moved.

"You've built up barriers between us, my love. I would have thought we would be past all these worldly obstacles by now."

The shadow grunted as he struggled to open the door. A couple of desks and chairs fell. Their clatter echoed in the classroom and down the hallway.

"Help!" Lumikki screamed again.

Outside, it was snowing. Light, soft, white snow. The first real, beautiful snowfall this winter.

"No one will hear you," the shadow said.

But there was uncertainty in his voice. That gave Lumikki's lungs additional strength. The shadow pushed his way into the room, but didn't turn on the light. He wanted to remain a shadow in the darkness.

But Lumikki recognized him anyway. The fog swirling in her mind parted, and Lumikki realized who her stalker was.

Henrik Virta. Her psychology teacher.

This realization startled Lumikki. How could Henrik have gotten so much information about her? And how could such an empathetic and friendly seeming teacher be so insanely cruel? Lumikki didn't have time to mull these questions over, though, because Henrik was shoving the desks and chairs out of his way in a rage.

"You fucking temptress!" he yelled. "Why are you doing this to me? I only want to love you and protect you. To keep you safe from everything. We are the same soul, you and I."

Lumikki grabbed a stapler and threw it at Henrik with all her strength. He managed to dodge at the last second and the stapler clattered against the wall.

"You missed," Henrik said, satisfaction in his voice.

"Just like you missed in your psychological evaluation of me," Lumikki couldn't help saying. "There isn't anything that's the same about us. You have never known me and you never will. And that isn't love anyway. That's just a sick obsession."

Lumikki's fear was gone. It had disappeared the instant she recognized Henrik and knew that he had never seen her deepest thoughts and feelings. Lumikki's core, her heart, was beyond this man's grasp. He would never reach her.

"If I can't have you, no one else will either."

Henrik's voice had turned quiet and low. Lumikki knew he was serious. He would kill Lumikki if he could.

A three-hole punch. Lumikki hurled it at his head. This time, it was too big to dodge and the sharp corner of the hole punch hit Henrik in the temple. He raised his hand and touched his face in surprise.

"Now blood is flowing from somewhere besides my heart," he whispered.

The melodrama was nauseating. It was as if Henrik believed he was in some kind of play where he had to deliver the darkest, moodiest lines he could invent.

"Help!" Lumikki shouted again, her voice now hoarse.

Henrik pushed the last desk out of his way. He could have his hands on Lumikki with a few short strides.

"You can't get away," he growled. "I don't understand why you don't give in to me."

Never, Lumikki thought and climbed onto the windowsill.

"What are you doing?"

Henrik suddenly sounded frightened.

Lumikki scooted to the edge of the windowsill. Then she lowered herself down the outside, hanging from the cold ledge. She glanced down. It was a long way down. Too long. But she didn't have any other options.

"Don't be crazy!" Henrik exclaimed.

"You're the crazy one here," Lumikki replied.

Lumikki felt Henrik's hands grabbing at her finger-tips, but she had already let go and was falling toward the earth with snowflakes swirling all around. She tried to relax as much as possible when she landed on the stone pavement below.

As she lay on her back in the newly fallen blanket of snow, Lumikki marveled for a moment that she didn't seem to have broken anything. Snowflakes swirled around in perfect minuets, dancing on her face and melting on her cheeks.

Then the pain came.

THURSDAY, DECEMBER 28,
TWO WEEKS LATER

19

First, Lumikki only moved her arms. Slowly, with long, patient strokes, she swept them up to her ears and then back, almost to her ribs. The snow was fluffy and soft. It moved as easily as she did. Then she remembered you were supposed to move your legs too.

It had been so long since she had done this. Since she was a child. Before she started school? Probably. During elementary school, the bullies had dumped her in snow-drifts so many times that the thought of lying down in the snow voluntarily wasn't the slightest bit appealing.

Snow angel.

The name was beautiful even though all it really meant was the depression her body left in the snow. Wings that the movements of her arms had formed. The gown her legs had shaped.

Snow angel. Lumikki and Rosa used to fill the yard with them. Before going to sleep, Rosa would tell Lumikki a bedtime story about the flock of angels that would descend from heaven during the night to sleep in the beds the girls had made for them. Rosa had said she was going to stay up to see the arrival of the glowing beings. Lumikki had made her sister promise to wake her up. Rosa promised and took Lumikki by the hand. And so Lumikki slipped into sleep with Rosa's warm hand gently holding hers.

Tears ran down the sides of Lumikki's face toward her ears.

More memories came every day. It was like she had a dresser inside her full of numberless drawers. One by one, the drawers were opening. All the drawers that had been locked for so many years.

Once upon a time, there was a secret girl.

Once upon a time, there was a girl who wasn't.

Now Rosa wasn't secret anymore. And although she had died, she still existed in memories and photographs and stories people told. She was no longer erased from existence. Grasping that her sister's entire existence had been concealed from Lumikki was still difficult. It was so appalling. She would never be able to accept her parents' decision.

They had made it in a state of shock, crazy with grief and trauma. Lumikki's parents really had believed Lumikki killed Rosa. By accident, yes, in the course of a game. Jennika's statement supported that and the child psychologists weren't able to get anything out of Lumikki that contradicted that version of events. Apparently, Lumikki had just talked about how they were "playing death."

Lumikki's father and mother had thought that carrying that kind of guilt would have been too great a burden for a child. That was why it was just better to shut that part of the past away. Lumikki thought that really it was more a question of her parents' inability to face their pain. Their daughter had been taken away. For them, it was easier to think that she had never existed. They simply rejected the truth because they couldn't endure it.

So they created a new, single-child family. They had destroyed almost every trace of Rosa. Only the photographs still existed, stored in the girls' former treasure chest. They had moved away from Turku. They had sworn the entire extended family never to breathe a word about Rosa. A vow of silence. A family of secrets. It was incomprehensible that it had worked. At first, Lumikki had asked about her sister, but when no one answered or they just kept saying she didn't have a sister, she eventually stopped. Her dad and mom had thought that she would forget because children do so easily. And in a way, she had forgotten for many years.

But the past can't be erased so easily. Everything leaves a mark on a person.

Everything surrounding the death had made her father unable to work for a while. First, he had traveled alone to Prague to think about what he wanted out of his life. They had considered divorce. Lumikki was only hearing about any of this now, a decade and a half after the fact. The family's financial situation had collapsed, which was why they didn't have the money to live in a big house like they had in Turku. They became a family where the most important things were never said out loud. They had become a façade of a family.

CHRISTMAS EVE, FOUR DAYS EARLIER

Lumikki sat on the couch and looked at the mantelpiece. Now, in addition to one daughter's picture, there was also one of them both together. As it always should have been. Mom brought her more mulled wine. They had just finished their Christmas dinner a little while earlier.

Her mother gently, tentatively touched Lumikki's hair. There were more words in that touch than there could have been in any long monologue. This touch was an apology for all the years when her mother hadn't known how to be a real mother.

Silent night, holy night
All is calm, all is bright

Round yon virgin, mother and child
Holy infant, tender and mild
Sleep in heavenly peace,
Sleep in heavenly peace.

Dad hummed along with the song. Lumikki saw the tears running down her father's cheeks. It was the first time she had ever seen him cry. Or at least, the first time she could remember. Maybe the time would come when, at moments like this, it would be natural for Lumikki to stand up, walk over to her father in his armchair, and hug him long and hard. But not yet.

They were still a silent family. Years of not talking didn't go away in a couple of weeks. Now there was a completely different, more peaceful, honest tone to the silence. It wasn't oppressive or suffocating anymore. The silence didn't stop up Lumikki's mouth and strangle her throat. She could breathe. She could be at rest and trust that the words would come in time.

When Lumikki fell from the window, a man walking his dog had just been passing by the school. He immediately called an ambulance and Lumikki was rushed to the hospital. She had come through with surprisingly few injuries, just bruises and sprains, nothing broken. She was forced to wear a neck brace for a week, but that was minor.

When her father and mother came to the hospital, Lumikki told them everything. A wave of relief washed over the sterile hospital room when Lumikki's parents learned that Rosa's death really had been an accident. They contacted Jennika, who after all these years was also relieved that she could finally tell the whole truth. The lie had weighed on her.

Rosa's death had been a tragic accident, and no one was to blame. What-ifs were never going to bring her back. Understanding and accepting that helped everyone touched by the tragedy. Piece by piece, step by step, they could take the repressed past back into their lives and make it a part of themselves.

Lumikki tasted the spices in her warm mulled wine. Cinnamon, cloves, ginger. She looked at the slow, dreamy motion of the straw mobile hanging from the ceiling. Outside, white snow was falling. The Christmas album they were listening to would soon be over and it would be time to go to sleep.

Lumikki knew she would sleep a long, long time, deeply, without any nightmares, in complete safety.

Lumikki continued making her snow angel, improving the shape of the wings. She thought of Henrik.

Her shadow. Her stalker. An obsessed man the depth of whose manic insanity had only been revealed after he was caught. When Lumikki fell from the window, Henrik fled to his home. Two hours later, the police broke the door down. They found Henrik unconscious on the bed.

He had taken an overdose of sleeping pills, but hospital personnel succeeded in reviving him.

At first, they hadn't found anything incriminating in his apartment, but then it turned out he'd built himself a "Lumikki room" in his storage locker in the building's attic space by covering the chicken wire walls with cardboard so no one could see inside.

When authorities were finally able to interrogate him, they found that his obsession with Lumikki had begun immediately after she started at the high school. Henrik's girlfriend had suddenly left him, and his mental health had collapsed. He had noticed Lumikki, who stood out from the other students, and fallen in love. Henrik had begun hoarding information about her.

He was astonishingly patient, persistent, and devious. He interviewed people at her previous school. He got wind of the bullying from some of Lumikki's old classmates. Next, he set about finding the names of her bullies and the extent of what they'd done. Henrik knew how to make an impression on people: He was calm, charismatic, and credible. Sometimes he posed as himself, sometimes as a reporter, and sometimes as Lumikki's school counselor or therapist. People trusted him.

Henrik found out who Lumikki's relatives were. At the end of a night out drinking, Lumikki's father's cousin, Mats Andersson, finally revealed that Lumikki had had an older sister who died. Using every possible skill and connection he had, Henrik ultimately succeeded in getting his hands on the police report about Rosa's death.

There were always people who knew people. Finland was a small country. If you wanted to know something, you just had to be determined and cunning enough. Henrik's psychopathy bent all of his intelligence and charm relentlessly toward his goal.

When Lumikki started dating another student, it spurred Henrik to action. His obsession grew by leaps and bounds. His desire to have Lumikki for his own had no limits, and he would stop at nothing to get her. He wanted to know everything about Lumikki, to own her, to control her with what he knew. It was all part of Henrik's power game.

Henrik had spied on Lumikki. He had followed her. Stalked her. Henrik had tracked Lumikki's every movement. His most brazen act had been going to talk to Lumikki's parents. Telling them that he also worked as the high school psychologist, he reported that Lumikki had visited him several times, talking about having dark thoughts. Henrik had made Lumikki's parents swear not to tell Lumikki about his visit. On the same visit, he stole the key to the treasure chest, the location of which a drunken Mats Andersson had revealed.

Lumikki didn't even know everything Henrik had done. And she didn't want to know. The most important thing was that he was in prison now and couldn't stalk her anymore.

Opening night of *The Black Apple* was postponed, but the show went on, one day before Christmas break. Lumikki had wanted them to still put on the play despite what had happened. She acted her role wearing the neck brace, pantomiming the glass coffin, and in the end, the show was better than anyone could have hoped.

It was an important night for Lumikki. It did her good to see that the images of massacre Henrik had threatened would never come to pass. They only existed in his sick imagination, and would never become reality.

The snow didn't feel cold under her back. Not yet. Lumikki decided to stay in her snow angel for a while and look at the bright starry sky that arced over her—dark, distant, and full of points of light.

She didn't believe that people turned into angels after they died. She didn't think that Rosa was somewhere out there looking down on her and watching over her life. Lumikki had a hard time thinking about the possibility that there could be life after death, at least in any form like this current one.

That thought didn't feel bad or sad. This was just how it was. Human life had a certain duration, a beginning and an end, and between the two, there was an amazing amount of space. Every breath contained more than anyone could imagine.

Lumikki knew that if she had chosen to, she could have been lying in the snow right now hand in hand with Sampsa.

And if she had chosen to, she could have been lying in the snow right now hand in hand with Blaze.

Lumikki's hands were empty. She was alone.

She had been forced to tell Sampsa that she couldn't keep seeing him. She had really liked him and gotten along great with him and even loved him in a way. But Sampsa had never seen deep into her thoughts and the shadows of her forest. Sampsa couldn't have seen, because for him those things didn't exist. His world was different, full of light.

Lumikki had also been forced to tell Blaze that she could never go back to him. She had loved him, and she loved him still, passionately, with all her heart. Blaze saw her completely. But Blaze was also able to hurt her so deeply that Lumikki could never expose herself to that kind of danger again.

But the biggest reason that Lumikki had needed to say goodbye to both Sampsa and Blaze was that she didn't trust either of them completely. She had thought either of them could have been her stalker. Even though it was only for a fleeting moment at the amusement park and even though her doubts had disappeared soon afterward. Still, those doubts told her that she didn't trust either with all her heart. How could she be with someone she didn't trust? How could she look either of them in the eye? A person she had imagined even for a second being capable of that kind of evil and cruelty? No one should have to be with anyone who had thought about them that way.

The tears continued running down her face. Lumikki let them flow freely.

She cried for many reasons at once.

She cried for her dead sister, whom she hadn't been able to mourn for all these years.

She cried for her family, which would never have the kind of warm, intimate bonds of trust that families should have.

She cried because she had been forced to give up happiness and love.

She cried because she was alone.

The stars in the sky suddenly felt closer. The light of those distant, twinkling suns was comforting. The universe was enormous. Lumikki's tears stopped flowing. Suddenly, she felt better. She was so small compared to everything. In this universe, everyone was alone in the end, but no one was alone. Everything was made of the same elements. Lumikki was just as strong and weak as crystals and rocks, waves and reeds, grass and rotting leaves, the burning heart of the sun and the cold void of space.

She had just as many layers and branched in just as many directions as a fairy tale a thousand years old. One that had started long before the words "once upon a time" and which would continue long after the words "and they lived happily ever after." Because nothing really happened only once. All stories existed many times, morphing and changing. And no one lived happily ever after. Or unhappily. Everyone lived happily and unhappily, both at different times and sometimes both at once.

This was Lumikki's universe. In its darkness and light was room for passion and fear, despair and joy. The air that filled her lungs was heady. In the embrace of the sky, she became more whole. She became more herself. She was free. Lumikki pressed her palms against the snowy ground and wished that she could become one with the freshly fallen flakes, merging with their infinitude.

A gentle night breeze blew through the park, moving the black branches of the trees and their shadows on the snowdrifts.

The world sighed and throbbed around Lumikki with one single pulse. Her pulse.

Photo © 2012 Karoliina Ek

ABOUT THE AUTHOR

Winner of the 2013 Topelius Prize, Salla Simukka is an author of young adult fiction and a screenwriter. She has written several novels and one collection of short stories for young readers, and she has translated adult fiction, children's books, and plays. She writes book reviews for several Finnish newspapers, and she also writes for TV. Simukka lives in Tampere, Finland.

ABOUT THE TRANSLATOR

Owen F. Witesman is a professional literary translator with a master's in Finnish and Estonian area studies from Indiana University. He has translated over thirty Finnish books into English, including novels, children's books, poetry, plays, graphic novels, and nonfiction. His recent translations include the novels in the Maria Kallio series, *My First Murder, Her Enemy and Copper Heart* (AmazonCrossing), the satire *The Human Part* by Kari Hotakainen (MacLehose Press), the thriller *Cold Courage* by Pekka Hiltunen (Hesperus), and the 1884 classic *The Railroad* by Juhani Aho (Norvik Press). He currently resides in Springville, Utah, with his wife and three daughters, two dogs, a cat, and twenty-nine fruit trees.